STAR CHAMBER

Antony James

PNEUMA SPRINGS PUBLISHING UK

First Published in 2009 by:
Pneuma Springs Publishing

Star Chamber
Copyright © 2009   Antony James
ISBN: 978-1-905809-56-1

This is a work of fiction. Names, characters, places and incidents are either products of the author's imagination or are used fictitiously. Any resemblance to actual events or locales or persons, living or dead, save those clearly in the public domain, is purely coincidental.

Pneuma Springs Publishing
A Subsidiary of Pneuma Springs Ltd.
7 Groveherst Road, Dartford Kent, DA1 5JD.
E: admin@pneumasprings.co.uk
W: www.pneumasprings.co.uk

A catalogue record for this book is available from the British Library.

Published in the United Kingdom. All rights reserved under International Copyright Law. Contents and/or cover may not be reproduced in whole or in part without the express written consent of the publisher.

STAR CHAMBER

Is this what it is going to take
to make our streets safer, to stop the mindless violence and disrespect?

Is this what it is going to take
to make them drop the knife and the gun?

Is this what it is going to take
keep our young people safe?

TERRY CHAPTER 1

*T*his isn't how it was supposed to be, we had a mission, fate had bestowed it on us. Only now it felt like fate had given us a dummy hand, set us up. I certainly didn't think things would end like this, I had felt noble like I was ordained by a higher power to flex my muscles and brainpower to devise such a thing. Now things seem to be crumbling around me my pedestal has been knocked and now I am teetering on the brink waiting to fall off, but scrambling hard to find my balance and stay upright. I have now to find a way to stay upright and see this plan through to the end, whatever that may be.

There were three of us, we knew each other from school and we were best men at each other's weddings, godfathers to each other's children. You could say that we were close, we didn't live in each other's pockets, but more often than not Friday night Saturday night saw us together either in the pub or at one of our favourite clubs partying hard, drinking hard or just chilling and chatting about all things, putting the world to right. Reminiscing about the good old days and how respect was a thing of the past, how kids of today didn't know the meaning of the word, didn't know how to behave. What we would do to them and so on. We had all lived normal lives, as normal as any life could be, Married, kids, jobs, mortgages we walked the walk and talked the talk. We read the newspapers listened to the news reports, and even saw these incidents at first hand. Black on Black crime, shoot outs in the streets, kids getting blown away for just looking at someone wrong. Drug deals gone wrong or just plain disrespect.

We heard the excuses and heard society washing its hands of the problem.

"It's a Black thing, as long as it stays in their areas let them sort it out..!"

"I grew up in a broken home, no father figure to put me right, no one to look up to, every man I knew was either a gangster, druggie or in prison, what do you expect me to do?"

Something had to be done; we couldn't sit idly and let it happen we wanted to be involved set the kids on the right path and away from this lawlessness. Terry was the oldest in the group, tall and gangly standing at 6" 4', fair skinned, even though he was 42 years old he looked ten years younger. He had been shaving his head for five years now mainly to hide the receding hairline and ever growing bald patch. An affliction he had inherited from his father. Who rather than keeping his hair short to hide the loss of his hair kept it long in a seventies afro style, however the afro grew at the side and back, his crown was hairless apart form a few wisps of grey making his head look like a well kept garden with herbaceous borders.

Terry had decided long ago that he would give something back to the community by working with the youths. He worked with them trying to show them the right path. He felt that he owed the community something having been, as a teenager, just like many of the youths he was trying to save now. He had sold drugs; he had his own little empire of runners feeding his regular and not so regular clients. When not drug dealing he was thieving to a grand scale, not just street robberies, but burglaries too. Although, he always said he didn't do this on his own doorstep to those who didn't have much, his patch was Knightsbridge, Chelsea and places like that. He had got so good at it that he only stole to order. If you had the cash and wanted a top spec surround sound stereo, or a high spec all singing and dancing computer, Terry was your man, or 'Steppers' his street name. If you wanted a snort, or a pull, or a tab, whatever, see Steppers he'll get it for you.

In that crazy gangster type of way, his success was his eventual downfall. Everyone knew his name, which meant that it wasn't long before the Police, the Drugs squad, National Crime squad, Flying squad, became aware of him. His name was all over the street, some people were jealous; some just wanted their piece of the action. His downfall was quick and clinical, I visited him in the 'Ville and he explained how his little empire came crashing down.

Apparently, the various different squads had been watching him for weeks now; they had even put in orders and filmed him from making the deal to handing over the goods. At the same time another set had come to him for a big drugs buy. He didn't have the goods with him but had set up a day and time to deliver the order, no money was to pass hands they were to telegraph the money into one of his accounts in one of his pseudonyms, normally he would have one of his boys do the delivery, but because of the amount he'd decided to do it himself, "in case something went wrong!".

The drop off was to be in the car park of the Alfred Hitchcock on Whipps Cross Road in Leytonstone. It was nice and big and open easy to get into and easy to get out of. It was set for 2pm before the schools were out and the rush hour traffic, again easier to get away if things went wrong. He had got up especially early that day 9am so that he could collect the goods from the various places, then have his packers package them in readiness for 2pm. At 10am he checked his account the money was in.

"Your account has just been credited with £150,000 Mr. Angle you require any further assistance?"

He had picked up the various packages from his sources and was dropping them off to his packers, when he noticed a blue Ford Mondeo pulling from a side road, why that registered with him he does not know but it did. He thought he recognised the driver, but couldn't think where he knew a middle aged bearded white guy from, was he an old teacher, father of one of his babes. Not sure, but then again he couldn't care too much, he had to get this stuff dropped off.

All packed and ready for him it was 1pm just enough time for a quick drink. He had placed the goods into the boot of his car and went back inside, opened a bottle of Brandy poured out a double measure saluted to himself and took a large sip. He looked out his window and noticed another blue Mondeo cruise past this time although the driver was middle aged or looked middle aged he did not have a beard he still looked familiar, but Terry couldn't place the face, anyway he had some important work to do; one hundred and fifty grand's worth – no time to think about old faces.

Time to go, into the car, get out of the car check goods secure in the boot, back into the car, start the engine, seat belt on, indicate, check mirrors, start to pull out, brake hard a blue Ford Focus appears from no-where youngish white guy eyeballs him, eyeballs back, no time for a scene.

"gallang about you business, Cha can't be boddered wid him!!"

Indicate again, start to move out, successful, turn right, 100 metres turn left, 200 metres to roundabout 2nd exit off, cruise for a few hundred yards indicate left into the Alfred Hitchcock, just about to turn check mirrors.

"Raas blue Focus right behind me look like him want somting?"

Pull into the car park, seat belt off, door open, door won't open some ugly White boy has his foot on my door, look in mirrors two blue Mondeo's and a Blue focus squeezing me in, look out front window, three men with bullet proof vests standing in front pointing something at him, all of them screaming at the same time.

Terry said to this day he could not understand a word they said to him, his mind was racing, his eyes zipping from one group of men to the other trying to make out what they were saying. He even thought that they were Russian Mafia out for him, they sounded Russian, and he had heard that they were muscling in on a lot of people. It dawned on him that it was police when his door was wrenched open a warrant card was shoved in his face. Finally he could understand them.

"You're nicked Son; you're gonna be spending lots of time at Her Majesty's pleasure!"

We were all there when he went down twelve years, twelve bloody years. His Barrister told us he got off lucky the normal tariff is fifteen to twenty Terry got time off for his early plea. I doubt that given the circumstances he could have pleaded any differently.

When he came out he was changed, he seemed more focused. He had seen lots of things that would make your skin crawl in prison he had got through them and came out the other side determined to be different. He had had plenty of time to think on his life and decided he had been selfish and needed to give back to the community something he felt he had not done in the past, which is why he went into community work. He really did care about these kids, he gave up most of his time for them, shaking his head on occasion when recounting some story about a crap little life.

When he would come out with us he would tell us stories of young teenage girls being raped by boys who were barely teenagers. Stories of initiations into gangs, how the older boys would surround themselves with nine to eleven year olds, who did their bidding. If the older boy had a beef rather than him getting his hands dirty he would set it up for these younger ones to settle it for him. They behaved like a pack of wild dogs, never one on one always ensuring that their prey was outnumbered to ensure victory.

He also talked about his success stories, he would always be amazed that amidst this wild uninhibited behaviour some managed to break away and become what you could call 'born again' respectable members of the society. This inspired him to carry on and he made it a point to use these success stories as an example to others of what can be achieved by all even in the most difficult situations.

Terry had been married to Eva for about three years, almost as soon as he came out, I was his best man, he had a daughter named Angelina. He and

Eva were as different as chalk and cheese. She had some high powered job with one of the large department stores. She was the director of something or other and spoke as if she went to Rodean rather than one of the local comprehensives. Terry – well he was street, earthy, roots. She was 5 foot 4 inches two shades darker than him, and very pretty, even at nine months pregnant she turned heads, she certainly turned Terry's head. They had met during his 'Steppers' days she had bought 'something' for a friend, they got chatting and the rest is history.

Angelina came within twelve months of his leaving prison. Eva had waited for him, religiously driving up to Warren Hill twice a month to see him. He would say that her visits kept him sane; she would arrive and pull out her list of things to talk about and proceed to cover every subject on the list. Terry didn't mind he just wanted to look at her, hear her voice and smell her perfume. He had vowed to make everything right with her when he came out, which he did. First the daughter then the wedding of her dreams. He had some funds stashed which the State didn't seize and used this to fund the wedding.

Recently, I began to detect that Terry was becoming frustrated with the youths, it wasn't enough to have the few success stories, he felt that we were losing the battle, that they were becoming a lost generation. Lost in the mists of drugs, disrespect, guns, knives, no honour, greed and down right laziness. We would talk for hours discussing what we would do to make it right. He felt the youth had no hope of a bright future and they needed to be given something to look forward to in life.

Terry would always lament the lack of role models to which these youths could look up to and try to emulate.

"Cha man, all dem see is dem rappers wid de slack lyrics drinking Champagne and fancy brandy, or de drug dealers' wid de fast cars and gyal all over de place. De fast life is all dem want. Dey can't play football and don't want to work hard cos it teks to long fe get dem tings. So what dey do, sell drugs, rob and burgle, easier dan working!"

My point would be to argue against this, I would tell him that there were more than enough role models today, especially when compared with when we were growing up.

In those days you hardly saw a black face on the telly and if you did he was some kind of awful caricature, if they were positive in any way they'd end up dead before the film or programme was half way finished. It is crazy to suggest that we didn't have role models in our community, and what was wrong with looking up to someone who has worked hard to get where they were. I'll tell you the problem; there're enough role models but they're scared to raise the heads above the bunker. Why? Because they'll have their heads shot off. They'll go down and try and help these youths but will come face to face with bitterness, jealously and bile. They'll get called all kinds of names, Uncle Tom, Oreo, sell out, even before they can get any sort of message across, then they'll find their nice car, mobile phone, themselves becoming targets for these poor misguided miscreants. I'm not buying into this mentoring role model crap.

Terry's angry reply would normally be to maintain his view and try to convince me that these people had nothing to fear as there were people like him who would offer them support and wanted them to stand up and be counted, make their voices heard and be a good example.

However, recently he began to ask different questions, questions to which none of us had the answers to, or so we thought. We were going through a transition which led to where we are now. I'm not sure why we didn't see it then, as it seems so clear now. What was needed was not more question and answer sessions but action and that action needed to be extreme.

"What is it that we is doing here man, we just talking the talking. What do you want to do about it? Me I want to go to dem people, to dem homes, dem workplace, dem fancy cars an' drag dem out. I want to take Shequira, talisha, Deon, with me show dem how dese people live, start de talking, get the uneasy introductions out de way. Would dis work, I don' know man, but to hear you say dem tings seem to say dem pickney dem is an underclass and haf fe stay in dere underworl'. That dese 'working' black people can den wash dem hands of dem and it becomes 'societies' problem not deres. But it is all we problem cos someday dey will break out from dis underworld and threaten not just de working black man but society too. Raas man, most a dese pickney dem is blood to dese people, so how you can turn you back on dem?"

JEREMIAH *chapter 2*

*T*he Third man in our little group was Jeremiah or Jerry, or 'The African' as Terry always called him. He was tall, not as tall as Terry, and dark, handsome and warrior like. His eyes were bright and smouldered seemingly to set on fire anything he gazed upon. Terry gave him this name after watching Roots as a term of endearment for what 'his' people went through before they became 'our' people. Jerry was very conscious about his African roots, but he also embraced everything about the Caribbean culture. He loved the music, the food, but more than anything else he loved women. Even at forty-one he was a 'playa' had no intention of settling down and played the field with a burning passion. He had three children from three different women, his oldest was Nelson just turned sixteen and as passionate about women as his father. His other children were girls, Tiana was 14, medium height and fair like her Mother, but she had inherited her father's eyes, and Alicia only 5 but knew it all.

Jerry was always well dressed suited and booted or casual in the latest designer wear. He stood out in any crowd and his eyes seemed to be a beacon for women to flock round and he loved it. He worked as a sports agent and had many well known sports men and women as his clients. This meant that he could get us into some of the best parties in town, rubbing shoulders with the rich and famous. He was at ease with these people, never star struck; he always seemed to know what to say and do in such vaunted company.

During our many chats he would remain quiet for long periods just listening to Terry and me. He always seemed more interested in watching other people in the bar or the latest group of girls that would walk in. As always they would notice him and whilst Terry and I would debate he would have sorted out in his own mind who his latest conquest would be. Never daunted; whilst we talked he would say his goodbyes and leave with her, preferring female company to trying to sort out the problems of our community.

*R*ecently, he began to listen more intently and make his views known more forcibly. He would argue that what these youths needed was some good old fashioned African or Caribbean discipline. He would argue that it wasn't about respect because you had to earn respect.

"Listen, I can't respect no man looking down the barrel of a gun or at the point of a knife. Yeah if he pointed his knife or gun at me I would say sorry and would mind my p's and q's but that ain't respect. I ain't scared because I'm looking at him remembering who he is and working out how I'm going to raas him up next time I see him. That ain't respect. Respect is what I have for my father, my uncles and the like. When they tell me to jump I would ask how high, if they tell me that the sky was green I would not argue with them, they are my elders. If I tried to talk back at them I would feel the back of their hand or I would have to go fetch the switch and my father would lash my arse. These kids need some good old fashion lashes that would put them on the straight and narrow."

I would argue with him that all this beating stuff was old hat, that we were now moving into the next millennium and that we needed new millennia thinking for a problem that has not yet been sorted out.

One of his responses really did get me thinking about where I stood in all this and whether my mind set needed to change.

"Listen you see all dese children, not just Caribbean, but African and Asian alike. They need one thing to make a difference for them. One thing that will sort them out from early and steer them clear of some of the shit that is going on today. Look now, if you live in one road or another estate you can't go across the road or to another estate without you getting into some beef, what kind of shit is that. Listen these pickney dem need one thing **DISCIPLINE**. And if their parents and peers aren't giving it to them then it has to be meted out by the state, or society. The only problem is the state and society ain't doing nothing.

I've thought about this long and hard man, it's the same as in America as in France, they believe that if they Ghettoise a problem it will stay there, they make certain laws and do certain types of policing that keeps the problem in check, and in the ghetto. It becomes a problem when it gets out of the ghetto and into homogenised white middle class areas.

Listen man, where are the guns coming from, where are the drugs coming from, who controls all this. It ain't that kid down the road nor the big shot over there, I'll leave you to think about that cos to tell you the truth I do not know the answer, but I am sure it ain't little ghetto hood over there!"

Invariably, he would then stay quiet listening to the rest of the conversation and studying the bar for something more interesting than what we were talking about. It made Terry and I think hard, Jerry's input always did, he was very much of the old school where discipline and corporal punishment were the main tools to bringing up your children, especially your male children. To an extent I agreed with him, because the discipline I had did not hurt me and made me into the person I am today, or so I believe. However, I always saw this as old fashioned. I could not see myself raising my children in that manner. My wife and I have always been more likely to embrace spock or super nanny methods, and the naughty step has been worn out by many bums squatting there for many minutes of many days. Our kids, I believe are well mannered and well behaved, intelligent, and respectful therefore it can be done without beating them up.

Jerry however has always been a stern father especially with Nelson, many a time I've looked on disapprovingly as he has laid into the poor boy beating him up and down the stairs for what I thought was a small indiscretion. I've been there at times when he has squared up to the boy, looking down on him raising his big hand and slapping him hard around his face, because he failed to say hallo when a big person entered the room. He was a little easier on the girls, but they didn't seem to challenge him ever, I did think that Tiana was scared of him, but there was a lot of love and respect for him from all of them.

We used to get into a discussion about Nelson mainly and how he was with him. I would try to get him to see that he needed to step back a bit and give the boy some space. He would retort that it was because these boys had too much space that they were wild like feral children.

"Listen mate, he needs a firm hand to guide him to wherever it is that he wants to go and to remind him that if he strays off the 'right' path then that firm hand is there to guide him back. I ain't giving up on him and I am going to guide him for as long as possible. You think I'm too hard on the boy. Look he's sixteen now and he's gonna have to make his own decisions, but believe me they will be based on what I have been trying to teach him about life. If sometimes it takes a slap around the head then so be it I'll carry on".

When I was growing up it didn't hurt me, the boy is lucky it's only me slapping him when I was younger it wasn't just me dad but uncles as well and friends of mum and dad would clip me round the ear for being rude or doing something wrong. Then they'll tell my parents and I'll get home and get another beating, that's what I mean by discipline, man. It shouldn't just be left to the parent but everyone should be involved because all of us have a stake in the future of these kids, because they will, inevitably shape our community; they are our future. This is the way things were in Africa and I am sure it was the same in the Caribbean as well, so why aren't we doing it now.

Listen mate, if you see him doing wrong or being disrespectful on the street I want you to cuff him and cuff him hard, if he comes home crying that you or some other adult cuffed him then I'll cuff him again, because I care about his future and mine and you should too."

Even though I could not bring myself to "cuff him" what Jerry said made me think long and hard. He really did have this way about him – he did not say much and sometimes did not contribute to a conversation. He would sit on the periphery listening, looking around the room, 'sussing' out the occupants, eyeing up a pretty girl, or simply looking bored, but he would then contribute something which left everyone quiet for a while pondering the effect of what he had said; like a conversation about shades of black girls who looked best. Trouble was everyone had their own preference, Jerry said;

"Listen, it is not the window dressing that would keep you with her but what lies underneath. You shouldn't measure someone by how much melanin they have but, if you are shallow - what she gives you in bed, if you want a relationship - what she will offer your mind..."

Jerry always seemed more at home talking with women; he was a different person around women, urbane, debonair in control of the conversation. He seemed to have a knack of knowing just what to talk about to keep either one or a group of women enrapt in his conversation. When I am out with him he seemed to me like the pied piper and attracted women with his voice and his eyes. I suppose the fact that he was handsome and always well dressed helped as well. We'd be sitting at a table and before you know it two or three women will make themselves at home. Jerry would introduce me, but you could see that they were not interested in me; Jerry was the man, the star maker, the lover. I suppose if I wasn't now married I would ensure that I picked up any of his 'cast offs', those were the days we were all 'happy', but things have changed, even though Jerry hasn't Terry and I have had to. Love caught us up and brought us down, we now just support Jerry and his conquests in mind only. No more crazy deeds like in the raving days.

BARRINGTON *chapter 3*

My name is Barrington, everyone calls me Barry, which I prefer. Barrington makes me sound like a reggae artist. Mother insists on calling me Barrington.

"That is the name you were given, after your grandfather, it was good enough for him, can't understand why you would want to shorten it."

Shorten it, or anglicised it I have and I prefer it. It suits my life and style and is a bit more urbane. I'm a solicitor; I work for the Crown Prosecution Service prosecuting the very same guys I wax lyrically about saving. Every day I read some statement from victims of crime and try to bring the full weight of the law down on the perpetrators. Every day in court I come face to face with some kid with no respect for authority blaming all their recalcitrance on society. Listening to their lawyers banging on about how hard they have had it, how society had turned its back on them and left them to fend for themselves.

"Is it any wonder that they fell into a life of crime, my client comes from a broken home, pushed around from relative to relative, then onto social services, who didn't care whether he lived or died. My client has accepted his guilt and is now before you looking for a chance, from this court, to make a proper go of his life. A custodial sentence would be wrong; he is prepared to pay reparation, and given the chance move away from the life he has known up to now..."

Every day I hear this, you could almost dispense with defence closing because they all seem to say the same things, just tick the box on the statement more apt for your client. But my fight isn't with defence lawyers, it's the system that allows these types of statements and on many occasions believes it and lets these people go free to commit crime again.

"We have listened with interest to what your lawyer has put up in your mitigation and we are minded to take all this into account. We have read with interest the all options pre sentence report from the probation service and have noted that you are trying to put your life in order. With all this in mind we have decided not to proffer a custodial sentence."

A smile and a wink from the defence Lawyer, I shuffle my papers as loudly as possible so as not to hear the actual sentence given, why should I care I've done my bit, pushed as hard as I could for the silent majority of us who do not commit crime, besides I've got a trial starting in the next court in fifteen minutes and need ten minutes to re-read some of the evidence.

I've been prosecuting for ten years now. Started out as a defence solicitor working for some two bit defence practice struggling on legal aid. Out all night in the police station, then all day in Court representing thieves, sex offenders, street robbers, drug dealers, murderers, the whole stinking unwashed masses. Pushing hard at the police station for them to "let him off with a caution" or "you have nothing to charge him with". Then into court, reading the papers advising the client, urging the court to be lenient. Been there worn the tee shirt. I left private practice and joined the government not because of any moral responsibility, but because the money was better, I got a pension, 30 days leave, I didn't have to go to the police station, worked five days a week and went home when court finished or early if I was minded to.

Those sorts of terms and conditions came in handy now I am married with kids. My wife of six years is Nicolette a barrister practising family law representing the more wealthy divorcing parties, earning a lot more than me and loving her days on her feet in the High Court or doing some deal where her wealthy client secures even better terms from her embittered not now so wealthy ex husband. Many a time she has tried to persuade me to leave crime behind and move into the sanctuary of civil law, but crime is in my blood either defending or prosecuting I can't leave it behind.

Nicolette and I have two boys Antony who is eight and Adrian four, both boys seemed to get their looks from their mother, two shades lighter than me strikingly handsome, and the apples of my eyes. Developing their own personalities, but daddy's boys all the way. We had originally met at university and had a relationship of sorts, but this revolved more around our love of law and fighting each other for books. We lost contact shortly after university then met again four years later when I was defending one of her clients who had trashed his house after being served with divorce papers by his then wife. I managed to get him off with a fine and for him to attend some dubious anger management course being run by some government funded agency. We had lunch, then dinner after court and re-kindled our relationship.

At university I had no interest in crime wanted to do commercial and intellectual property and work for one of those big city firms. Armed with a 2:1 I majored in intellectual property, in which I bagged a 1st. I sent my C.V to every City firm looking for articles. I got interviews by the bucket load, was assertive, witty, charming, I exuded confidence, but I never got an offer of employment. I began to doubt myself, but remained strong but became more truculent and forceful, but still no job offers. I had never been a victim before, but I felt like one then, a victim because of my colour, that could be the only reason why these big boys were not letting me in. I didn't like the taste of victim and didn't have time to fight the powers although I carried on applying and getting interviews, but now I didn't want their job I went to make a point and confront these people who did their dirty work behind four lines in a rejection letter.

I changed approach and started applying in general law firms, the usual high street firms doing legal aid, a bit of this and a bit of that. I was offered a job on my second interview, the money was crap, but the firm seemed to be young and vibrant. I was assigned to a principal who did mainly crime work and that is where I stayed until I crossed over to prosecuting.

I knew that this move would not sit right with Terry, considering what he had been through and what he was now doing, trying to keep these kids out of trouble. However, I wasn't doing this for Terry or to salve any conscience he may have, I was doing this for myself and my family. It wasn't as exciting as defence work, but it was still engaging and interesting, and going by the state of the majority of the case papers, I had a lot of work to do on my feet in court.

Terry wasn't happy, when he first found out he was livid and we didn't talk for two weeks. He went through all the invectives spewed his bile on me about turning my back on the youths, setting them up for a fall, becoming the very Babylon that is locking up the youths.

"Man you just become Babylon, you is now part of the system that is keeping these pickney dem down. You can't be serious about dis can you? when one of my boys come against you what you gonna do wink at him and lose you papers, or say your honour give him life in prison, man I can't talk to you right now, what am I gonna say to dem youths when they ask me about dis, I don't know man, I don't know..."

Jerry was a lot more circumspect and just smiled as he listened to Terry's rant. For him it was a sensible move and in the mad scheme of things didn't really matter.

"Listen mate, it doesn't matter where on the top table you sit just as long as you are sitting there. If you are there then you can affect change. You can't effect change if you are not there or cannot be heard. Listen mate Terry will come round, don't worry..."

Typical Jerry always able to look at the bigger picture and in a sense he was quite right I was still there at the coal face and decisions made by me could make a difference to people, lots of people not just the villains but their victims as well. I could not lose sight of this and I did try to remind Terry of this, that for every crime there was more than one victim, that the large majority of people both in our community and out (black or white) did not commit crime and were more likely to be the victims of crime, that I had a duty to them even more so than the small minority of recalcitrants and recidivists.

After two weeks Terry called me up, he had been thinking long and hard about what I had been saying about my decision, he had also been talking with Jerry and Eva, who both told him to stop being silly and get off his laurels.

"Yeah man, I tink I was a little hard on you, but you gotta understand it was a bit of a shock. I kept seeing you as that snooty prosecutor in my case, the wanker tried to make me out to be the Black Caesar. I couldn't see beyond that, but hey I know you is a good lawyer and you will use your powers wisely. In fact, it could be a good thing for some of youths to come up against someone like you who understands the streets and what is going on. So man come for a drink and I'll be the last one to shake you hand."

We went out that night and got completely drunk, talking into the night and then getting kicked out of the bar just because Terry broke a few glasses trying to get up quickly to go to the toilet – well about twenty glasses. Somehow he managed to stumble over a table, knock down an old man's glass, he then stumbled back into a waitress carrying a tray of food the waitress and the food went flying into the manager, who had just stepped out from behind the bar and they all landed in a heap on the floor covered in the dish of the day plus prawn cocktail and two glasses of water. I managed to get Terry out of there and called Eva to pick us up, she was none too pleased at the sight of him, but happy that we were back as friends.

We did have many conversations about my work, Terry asking what happened to this person or that, or giving me a scenario and asking me what would be the likely outcome and sentence if one of his boys was caught for this or that reason. He became very interested in the types of sentences, especially those that did not involve jail. I would try as best as I could to explain the types of sentences and how they fitted the crime and whether it was best to confess at the police station or at court.

His interest increased when one particular boy he was having a lot of problems with at his community centre got arrested. I could see that this boy was troubling him; he had tried everything he knew to get him to see that he was heading for serious trouble. He had been arrested for minor offences in the past; loitering, threatening behaviour, possession of drugs, but these offences hid what he was really up to. Most of his family were involved with some sort of illegal act, brothers, cousins, uncles, even an auntie had all spent some time in prison or were sentenced to working on some community project or other. This guy was heading the same way and Terry saw it as his moral duty to try and sort him out, but he had resisted all his efforts.

JUNIOR SHOTTA chapter 4

"*M*e is a shotta man, you can't do nutting to I or I will blow you away man. Me nah get catch dem boys don't know me, dem can't touch me. Cha' I do what I want when I want and not a ting can judge me, scene."

His real name was Everton Weekes he was fifteen going on forty. He was brought to Terry's attention by his mother who had heard about the project Terry was working on through friends on the estate. She was anxious because she felt he needed to be turned away from the gangster lifestyle lived by his two older brothers and his uncles. He was the youngest in the family and she always thought that he would hold more promise and had strived to push him into education and making something of his life. But she was always afraid that the excitement and ready money of the life of his older siblings would tempt him. She had even thrown out his older brother Alton just so he could not influence him negatively, but it didn't work he was in it before she could blink and hanging onto his brother's coat tails as tightly as possible. She still had hopes for him, which is why she went to Terry.

"He's not a bad boy he's just been led astray by his no good brothers. I know he can do something else, but this world he's trying to get into he thinks is easier, he thinks he's getting respect but all he is is their little messenger bwoy, their younger running around doing their bidding. They are all deluded if they think they are going to make something of it, I'm scared he's going to end up like most of the others in prison for a long time or worse dead, talk to him please; bring my boy back!"

This was too much of a challenge for Terry, he asked her to bring him down to the centre and he will talk to him and see how things were. He knew his brothers especially Alton as Alton had worked for him for a while. He had a lot of respect for Alton because he wasn't in your face about what he did, he just got on with it, in fact, it was Alton who took over his 'patch' when he finally went down and had kept it going for many years without being caught.

Terry always said that Alton was probably smarter than him. Whereas Terry wanted the quick, big hit that could get him out of it, Alton had no illusions that he was ever leaving this life. For him this was it, what he was going to do was to build up his empire have the runners and the go betweens, expand into other areas then sit back and watch the money roll in. Alton had had a few scrapes with the police but never anything big, he set up the deals talked money, sorted out the drops, but never closed them, he had others who did that, he paid them well, frightened them as well, he had a mean streak, which meant he didn't mind cutting someone up if he even smelt that they were going to double cross him. He liked to torture them, taking his victim to his special lock up in the middle of an industrial estate. Inside was empty except for a small desk with a large desk lamp, a large workmate table fitted with straps, a large wooden chair again fitted with straps and most weird of all leather straps hanging form the ceiling light which shone down illuminating the workmate. On the desk was an array of tools, hammers, screwdrivers, pliers, jemmy's and a whip.

Everyone who was on the street had heard of the torture chamber, which after a few years had gained legendary status and given Alton a place in local folklore. Every week there were different stories about who had been invited to the torture chamber and what had happened to them, whether they were true or not they added to the fear and respect people had for Alton. There were even stories that he kept a collection of fingernails and toe nails of his victims, which he kept in large picture frames, against each was an entry with the name and date when they were forcibly extracted.

Terry also knew his other brother Ellis, he was dead now. Ellis was a real villain; he wasn't into drugs, but loved money, easy money. He had graduated from street crime and burglary to armed robbery. He was meaner than Alton the same vicious streak but more sadistic with it. He had been a football hooligan in the seventies and eighties running with the main groups supporting West Ham United. He got out of this after being arrested at nearly every football ground in the country. On a Saturday it seemed that every police force knew his name, which didn't help him with his day job.

He still had that bloodlust which he sated on a Saturday night in some pub or club. He'd drink seven or eight pints with his mates, getting louder and louder. By the time the sixth pint went down they would have decided which person or group they were going for and deliberately goad them. By the eighth pint all hell would break loose. Ellis would make sure he had at the least bottled someone by the time they got pushed out by the bouncers.

No one knew who had killed him, word on the street was that it was his crew that had pulled off the Docklands security van job that had netted something like three million pounds, a security guard had been shot and another stabbed in the neck just missing his jugular vein, the other guard was kicked senseless, apparently his whole body being one big bruise. Ellis hadn't been seen for a month after this, which added to the theories that he was behind it and that he was in the Caribbean somewhere living it large, drinking champagne, lots of women and eating great food. It came as a big shock when the morning papers blazed;

"Suspect in Docklands raid found dead on landfill site"

"A man subject to a major police manhunt, which included, controversially, officers from the robbery squad flying off to the Caribbean in search of him has turned up in London and was dead. His emaciated body was found by 'scavengers' at a London rubbish tip. Because of the decomposition of the body the actual cause of death is not yet known, however eyewitnesses have said that they had noticed many injuries consistent with him having been shot and stabbed numerous times. One of the local 'scavengers', so called because they spend their days looking for re-useable items from the rubbish tip and landfill site and selling them on at markets and car boot sales;

'I had just turned over this large cardboard box and thought bloody hell it ain't often you come across a black mannequin, but on second look I realised it was a body, it was naked and covered in blood and bruising, there were 'oles in him I think he was shot up, 'orrible it was, called the police and 'ere we are.'

Police have named the body as that of Ellis 'Notorious' Weekes. At the time of going to press no leads to his death have been discovered, a police spokesman confirmed that they will now start to question known associates in order to piece together his last known whereabouts.

Weekes has spent over half the last six years in and out of prison, apart form the Docklands raid he has been questioned before about a string of other armed robberies carried out in the East of London. He was also part of the infamous Weekes family. Operation Trident are investigating"

By mid afternoon the news had flashed back and forward around the streets, everyone in the underworld was talking about Ellis' death. Rumours ran like wild fire throughout the community as to who had killed him or what had happened to him. Many stories linked his death back to Alton and his infamous torture chamber. The word was that Ellis had indeed carried out the Docklands raid, but that he had gone too far by killing the guard. The raid was perfect, they got away with a lot of money, their intention was to lie low for a while, carry on as normal, but by killing the guards the other members of the gang knew that he had gone too far. It was Ellis who shot the first guard, he didn't stand a chance, he then set on the second guard kicking him senseless then for no reason whilst he lay helpless stabbed him in the neck, he would have cut him from ear to ear but was stopped by one of his gang. He then started on the third guard who was on his knees hands up with a gun to head when Ellis began kicking him until he was a twitching mess on the floor. It took two other gang members to drag him off and into the getaway van. Ellis had secured the torture chamber as the gangs resting place and it was whilst in there that he was set upon by the rest of the gang. Taking him by surprised they all jumped on him hitting him with anything they could find, then shooting him five times to make sure he was dead, then dumping his body at the landfill site.

The word was that Alton was made aware of this and had received 'compensation' for Ellis. Apart from money he had insisted on the other gang members leaving the area as he couldn't contemplate seeing or bumping into any of them, but he knew that his brother was a loose cannon and someday it would end like this. He wasn't about to make the same mistake as him and made sure his empire was run tightly and any indiscretion treated with brutal force, better them be scared of him than have no respect.

*T*his was the world that Terry was attempting to extricate Everton from. It excited him and, at the same time filled him with dread. When he was introduced to him he tried talking to him to see what made him tick, what he thought about, what he liked doing, but he got nothing just a blank stare and a kiss of his teeth. He tried talking to him about his mother and what she wanted for him, nothing again. He then mentioned Alton and how he knew him from back in the day. This caused a stir in him; his eyes widened a little looking right at Terry for the first time. Terry could see his mind working trying to link this youth worker with his gangster brother but couldn't make the connection.

"What you know about Napoleon man, how you can drop his name like you knows him. He don't run wid no pussy bwoys."

"Who you calling pussy bwoy, hear dis bwoy is me who did make Napoleon, you see his tings is me did run dem first, go an' ask him 'bout me den come back to me wid some respect!"

Terry let him go, he didn't want to reveal this much so soon, he wanted to ease into it and gain some respect from the boy for who he was now not what he used to be then. He knew that he would be back and probably looking at him in a different light might even be more amenable to what he had to say. The next day Terry was visited by Alton, who turned up at the centre in a Porsche 911 private number plates, parking in the centre manager's parking place and strutted into the centre demanding to speak with Terry. Terry greeted him with a smile and held out his hand, Alton refused it.

"Need to speak somewhere private, come not got long no time for all dis"

Terry took him to the meeting room, told him to take a seat and locked the door. He braced himself ready for anything that might come his way, he knew Alton, ran with him and taught him and as he was only talking with Everton the day before knew it had something to do with him. Alton didn't waste anytime on pleasantries and began to talk even before both of them were seated.

"So you've met my Ma and my little bro then. She's been on at me for months now not to bring him into all this. I've gone round there for Sunday dinner and she's wailing and shrieking about him going on like a gangster and ending up like Ellis, you know what I mean. She's sweating me big time to look after him and get onto the right path. Shit man, she's even threatening to stop cooking for me and you know that can't happen cos I love me Ma's cooking, Sunday ain't Sunday without her roast and veg and rice n' peas, you know what I mean. I can tell you cos you understand, you know, I didn't want him into all this, I've cuffed him 'nough times to tell him to go home. But, he was gonna get into it with or without me you know, just thought it better he's with me than one a dem other dudes who think dem is Shotta but can't handle it You know what I mean."

Terry was a little puzzled by this, he had expected Alton to come in all angry and banging tables, but he was quite humble and it seemed like he was looking for Terry's help.

"Ev needs to be out of this, you know what I mean, Ma is right, he's a bright kid, he was her one hope that one of her kids wasn't gonna let her down, you know. He was alright up until about a year ago, seems when puberty kicked in the rebel in him came out as well, you know. I've tried to make it easier for him by giving him little jobs, you know, some runnings here and there, you know, but it seems to have gone to his head. You've seen him, stubborn little bastard just like the rest of us, ha, ha ha you know what I mean man. If you can do this I'd be grateful, but if he doesn't turn away from this then he's back under my wing and I'll have to find a way to get me Sundays back in order, you know what I mean. I've spoken to him told him we go way back and that he should show you respect and listen to you, you know. Take him to talk to your Lawyer friend and the African, they kinda like got good jobs and earn a decent wedge. He's coming to you tomorrow, even if I have to bring him here myself, he'll be here, you know."

He was looking for Terry's help. Terry couldn't work out whether the main reason was his Mother starving him his Sunday roast or that he really did care about this kid's wellbeing. Terry agreed to try again and talk with him and that he would try and bring Jerry and I in as well.

"Nice one steppers, if there is anything I can do for you, you know, just let me know, you always did alright by me, never tried to dis me, you know, so call me hears me card."

He handed Terry his card, which Read "*Alton Weekes; Weekes Associates Imports, exports, fancy goods retail and wholesale*" Terry read it with a smirk on his face as he saw Enid and Beatrice from the Women's Institute accosting Alton because he had sold them Columbian ground cocoa beans rather than Columbian ground coffee beans.

Everton did turn up the next day on his own, he seemed quiet and reflective and greeted Terry with a yes sir, how are you. Although he didn't apologise for his behaviour the first time they had met, Terry understood that his attitude now was apology enough. Terry started talking to him by asking him a variety of questions;

Why do you do this?
What do you think you will get out of this?
What is it that you really want to do with your life?
What about school?
How are you getting on in your studies?
Who do you hang around with?
Who is your main man?

What is it that they do for you?
How would you feel if one of these guys was hurt?
What do you think you could do about it?
What if it was you?
Would anyone care?

Everton looked perplexed by the questions he had thought Terry was just going to talk at him, telling him how much of a good boy he was and a life of crime was not for him, to study and get good grades then he could struggle like everyone else. But these questions were different and they made him think for the first time in a while about his life, but he was stubborn.

"Cha man, wot you asking me all dem things for. Me and me crew are tight, no-one messes with us, besides everyone knows Alton is me brother so ain't no-one gonna mess with me, I will do things to them, hurt dem, black dem out if they want to trouble me cos me is original!"

"Yeah, yeah, Everton heard it all before, you are all original Shottas, you all do the same bloody thing. Yeah you got Alton, that makes you different, but how many others out there have brothers running things just like Alton. Your crew is tight, I've seen how tight crews are, and when the time comes you'll see how tight your boys are. Your mother don't want you doing this stuff, not even Alton, but he's your brother and he will look after you, but when he ain't around who's gonna help you?"

"Nah man he'll always be there, he's smart man ain't no-one gonna bodder him. You tell me where someone like me can earn this much dosh..!"

He went into his pocket and pulled out a stack of twenty pound notes waving them in Terry's face.

"I don't need this man I'm stacked and I got me crew and Alton will always give me work, why should I go to school and read Shakespeare and mess around with Bunsen burners, listening to some boring old stiff droning on about crap I got no interest in."

Terry simply smiled at him, thinking this kid was so far on the wrong track that it was looking impossible to bring him back, but he'll try for his mother's sake and for Alton to get his Sunday dinners back.

"Cha man I'm outta here got some honeys to sort out. I'll come back cos my brother tell me to, but you ain't said nuffing yet man, nuffing this life is cool, I got my honeys, I got the money, I got the lyrics and I got my crew. No one can touch this and I ain't giving it up for no books, see ya old boy"

With that he got up and bounced out the room head cocked to one side, trousers half mast, his last act was to pull his hood firmly over his head and then he was gone.

He came to see Terry on a regular basis once or twice a week for a month. Even Jerry and I met him talked to him, showed him what life on the other side was like. We thought we were making progress with him, he seemed to be taking it in, he seemed impressed that two guys from the hood were making serious money and rubbing shoulders with the rich and famous without doing something illegal. He seemed more attracted to Jerry, mainly because of the glamour of his job, and even spent a day at his office, meeting some of his vaunted clients. But, it all seemed too little too late, he was in the gangster lifestyle over his head, it was all he knew and it finally took him.

We woke up to the morning news, headlines blaring;

"Younger brother of the Docklands raider found beaten and stabbed to death behind a local youth club

Another death, another family coming to terms with their loss

Junior gangster found stabbed to death dead"

"A Mother loses another son to the badlands of the street. Everton Weekes 15, also known as Shotta was found dead behind the Catskill Road Youth Centre last night he had been stabbed three times. This brings the number to two the sons Mrs. Weekes has lost to violence in the last three years. The Police report that he was chased and cornered by two unknown assailants before being beaten up, stabbed and left for dead.

An eye witness who lives on an adjoining road, but does not want to be named reported hearing many loud shouts and the sound of someone screaming. On looking out his window he noticed a youth now known to be Weekes being chased towards the Catskill Road by two other youths. He immediately phoned the police, who on investigating the area found the body of Weekes. Police have not yet made a statement.

This brings to 35 the number of young men shot or stabbed to death on our streets this year and we are still only in September, when is this madness going to end, what are we going to do to stop this killing of our young. Operation Trident is investigating."

I met Terry and Jerry in the bar the same night, none of us spoke for a long while. We just sat looking into the bottom of our glasses. We all knew that one day he would end up this way, that what we were actually doing was trying to save his life, but we failed, he failed.

Later Terry told us that the word on the street was that Everton had roughed up some guy's sister, slapped her around and forced himself on her. She hadn't wanted to make a complaint because of who he was and knew that her brother would go out seeking him for retribution. It seems the brother found out and took out the ultimate retribution. Furthermore, this guy's parents had now shipped him out of the area some say to Birmingham, Manchester or even to the Caribbean, somewhere out of the firing line. There were many suggestions as to who was the second assailant but no one knew for certain.

ALTON Chapter 5

Alton was mad and very angry, he had lost his second brother to violence one he had control over, but this, he was the youngest, he had changed his nappies, bottle fed him, taught him to read, played games with. He took it bad, word was that he had his people scouring the streets everyday for news, they had pulled people into the torture chamber, but no-one knew where the perpetrators were. Many people were not talking because they despised Everton he had rubbed too many people up the wrong way with his mini gangster impressions. A number of girls started to come forward, mainly through the offers of cash from reporters to confirm how he had violated them.

"He was just fifteen but he was out of control, one girl described how he abused her then threw her to his 'crew' when he had finished with her. Before they let her go he had pushed a gun into her mouth to show what would happen to her if she talked. Life on our streets..."

His Mother had taken it very badly, the image of her on the television, crying, screaming, and wailing whilst being propped up by other female relatives was hard to stomach. Alton was always in the background looking on remorsefully but looking completely helpless. All his money and contacts couldn't keep his little brother safe. A few months after this his mother went back home to Jamaica, England had too many bad memories for her, since Everton's death all she would talk about was life back home, sitting on the veranda watching the day go by away from all this violence and ungodliness. Alton had taken her to the airport, had ensured she had enough money and that her house in Jamaica was ready, he couldn't do enough.

He had revealed to Terry that since Everton died she had not looked at him, simply sat in her chair by the window looking out as if she was watching Everton playing in the garden. Her last words to him before she boarded the plane was that she would pray for him, that was it and then she was gone.

Alton had many visits from the Police asking him for information, then warning him not to get involved, that if they had anything they would let him know, that he had to stop pulling people off the streets as this was their job. They threatened to bring him down if he sought revenge. Alton wasn't listening, but he knew that he and his gang were being watched, that is why he came to Terry.

"Steppers, I need your help man, you know. I'm being watched by dem man, I can't do nutting man, you know. Dis Everton thing it's hard you know, Mum's taken it real bad blaming herself, says she should have taken him away. Fuck man, she even told me she don't blame me, that she understands I was just trying to look after him, that fucked me up, you know what I mean? I need you to tell me what the word is on the street, who's being named. Don't want nothing more nothing less just the names. I heard about dis gyal, I know who she is, I know her brothers gone somewhere I'll get him later. Who was the other one? Man, this is so fucked up, what do I do, do I kill them, if I do, you know, it's another brother from the community dead, enough of them are already dying, but they took my brother. I know the work you're doing, don't this fuck you up as well?"

Terry didn't answer, he could see how all this had affected him. He wanted to tell him to leave it, to mourn his brother and get on with his life, but conversely he kept thinking what if it was his brother, his son what would he do. He would be on the streets every day looking, asking questions, but once he was face to face with them what would he do; could he pull the trigger? He probably could years ago during his dealing days, but now he was here to save a life not take one. He wanted to say to Alton, that he understood how he felt, but his brother was a little shit, what about those poor little guys scarred for life by him, do you know if he was responsible for at least one of those other 34 lives, and the usual clichés like 'if you live by the gun you will die by the gun. He could see in Alton's eyes and the way he was talking that he was thinking exactly the same, he didn't need a street preacher to tell him.

"You know, maybe I don't want to know, maybe I just draw a line under this and move on. I tried to protect him, but maybe it was my fault, I gave him things most fifteen year olds only dream about, he lived the bling lifestyle because of me, had his own hangers on, you know. Maybe if I had slapped him about and told him to piss off, you know what I mean, this is fucked up, real fucking shit, forget what I asked you, I'll see you later, know what I mean."

Terry just nodded and watched him leave, he seemed to have lost his usual swagger, he seemed smaller; his clothes looked like they were one size to big. All Terry could think was; "There goes a beaten man, beaten by the very life he chose for himself, thank God I got out of it at least I can sleep at night!"

Months past but no new leads came up regarding the perpetrators, the streets had calmed down and everything seemed to go back to normal. Even Alton was his old self and the revolving door of the torture chamber was working as hard as ever.

NELSON Chapter 6

*J*erry had been having problems with Nelson for a while now, his mother had been complaining to Jerry constantly about how Nelson had been staying out at night smoking, drinking and womanising. She had found a packet of Benson and Hedges under his bed along with four pornographic magazines and a box full of condoms. She was worried because if he was out he could end up like one of those other boys shot or stabbed lying in the gutter somewhere. Jerry had tried to talk to him, threatened to beat him, but nothing was working.

"Dad man you can't keep trying to run my life I'm sixteen now, so what if I smoke the odd cigarette or drink the odd drink, or even have sex occasionally, it ain't anything to worry about. Mum's just freaking because of what is happening on the streets. You know as well as I do that most of it is press sensationalist. I ain't in no gang, I ain't got no beef with no-one and I ain't running on the streets. We go to the Youth club then we hang out at each other's houses, the only time that we are on the streets is between home and the youth club. Lay off Dad, it may not concern you or Mum, but me and my girl have split up, I'm just drowning my sorrows, but I'll be back to normal soon."

"Listen, why didn't you tell me? What I'm worried about is your smoking and stuff, your mum tells me she found cigarettes in your room, but what about them?"

"Oh them! I tried them didn't like it chucked the box under me bed and forgot about them, was going to give them to Salisha when she came round, for her to give to her brother Tyrone, always meant to but we always got busy doing other things!"

"Ah and that as well, listen, I remember my time at your age, huh! Ha, ha, ha!"

Jerry had given a deep laugh, then patted his son on the back, trying to show his empathy. Yes, he remembered those days at sixteen when he chased anything in a skirt, black, white, Oriental, Asian, as long as it was female he chased it and chased hard. He imagined his son, the apple of his eyes repeating those conquests, like father like son. He was a little concerned to hear that he had split with Salisha as he knew how Nelson felt about her. Even at sixteen they looked good together and she came from a 'good family'.

He had asked Nelson what had happened between them. Nelson explained that she had said that she wanted to concentrate on her studies, didn't want a relationship clouding her path. She stopped taking his calls and on going round to her house her Mother told him that she had gone for 'a sabbatical' with her brother to their cousins who lived in Atlanta.

"Listen son don't worry she'll be back, but while she's gone and you're single you shouldn't be moping around go out and live boy."

Nelson simply shrugged his shoulders, said his goodbyes and left. Jerry thought for a while about his son's demeanour and the sudden split with his girl. He was a little concerned that he didn't seem that happy, but put it down to his age.

"Bwoy we was all a little flaky at that age one minute up next minute down, I don't think any of us really knew what was happening inside, but that's the path to manhood and we all go through it, just need those around us to understand it."

Jerry had told me that he and Nelson's mum had a row about it and how she felt that he had just ignored his son's problems. She was adamant that it was more than just Salisha going off, he wasn't around him all day like she was and she could see that things were on his mind, that the smoking and drinking were symptomatic of something going on. She had trusted Jerry to get to the bottom of it but as usual he couldn't see it, couldn't empathise enough with him to draw it out.

He had told her to give the boy a little space it was just growing pains that he's going through and it was nothing to be concerned with. When he is ready he'll let it out and get on. She just needed to give him space and get off his back.

On leaving his father Nelson breathed a sigh, there was so much that he wanted to tell his father. He wanted to entrust him with some of his secrets, unburden himself like a sinner at confessional, but he knew that it would do no good and cause more problems and problems bring to the fore the fist fight with his father that was always a hairs breadth away whenever they met up. They were becoming like stags, first the stand off, then lots of bellowing and false charges and finally horns lock, the battle commences. The young stag against the older more mature stag, who will win out, will youth flourish or will maturity win out, stay tuned. They were at the rutting stage and Nelson could feel a strange animosity for his father, he hated it when he compared him to himself at that age.

"I don't want to be like him, I am my own man, I have my own identity, I ain't Jerry the love god!"

He wasn't sure what he wanted from his father, maybe nothing, maybe something. Maybe he wanted him to just listen to him, hear his pain, understand what he is going through. Instead he felt patronised by him; he only wanted to talk to him because his mother said so, because she found some cigarettes and condoms. He wanted him to hear him say that he wanted to still be with Salisha but circumstances, events meant they had to be apart. He wanted to say to him that she was more than just a girlfriend she was his best mate, that she gave him the opportunity when they were together to be himself.

It made him think about who he was, immediately he said to himself that he wasn't Jerry, they shared the same gene pool, which he thanked his father for, but he was more than just Jerry's genes. He liked reading, not just Dickens, Shakespeare, Austen and the rest, but he had recently discovered Baldwin, Wright, Himes, Mosley, Achebe, Hurston, Walker, Angelou. Writers who were black, writing about 'The Black Perspective', writers he had not been introduced to whilst at School, but writers every bit as adroit and adept as their white counterparts, writers who seemed to understand him, who understood and explained to him where he was coming from.

He had tried to explain this to Jerry, have a discussion about these novels and the writers, but, as usual, Jerry remained quiet, listened to him and said; "Listen son, those guys were real good, read a few of those myself, but they ain't the real world. You can't simply read them and believe what they say is gospel the same way that you can't read white writers and accept them solely, you need to balance it. You ain't passing English Literature just on Baldwin's words, you understand?"

This had made Nelson angry, he felt that his father didn't understand the journey, nor did he believe that his father had been on this journey.

He liked sport, football in particular and represented the school and district, he also played for West Hams youth team and had hoped to sign professional, but had been persuaded by his mother to put his studying first. So he left West Ham at sixteen and signed for Leyton FC a semi professional side, which allowed him to carry on studying and playing at a reasonable level. He had recently got into the reserves and had been substitute for the first team on a couple of occasions. He really enjoyed this, a small club with a bit of ambition, which gave him the chance to pursue his options whilst studying. He played up front, normally the lone striker, because of his size. His best skill was his shot, hard and fast, he could strike a dead ball with both feet and was deadly accurate from the penalty spot. He led by example and never shirked a challenge, many times he got hurt but would never show his opponent that they had hurt him he was smiling at them as if to say, 'is that all you've got?'

A' levels that is all he heard from his mother and father, before that it was GCSE's, he knew after A' levels that they would drum into him university. His plan was to ensure he chose a university in the Midlands or up North to ensure his escape plan to get away from them, then he could really start living his life away from their prying, nagging eyes. He didn't mind studying; in fact he was quite happy with it. To him it was a lot better than working, now he was doing A' levels, he had a lot more spare time, which gave him the chance to hang out with Salisha and train with his team.

That was until she upped and went with her brother to somewhere in Atlanta. He understood why and he even pushed her into it on the basis that it was safer for her to be away from things for a while. She would be able to recuperate and get back to the person he knew. He could see her changing, she became introspective, not trusting anyone, for no reason she would burst into tears, she wouldn't let him close. Before, they used to enjoy a long and lasting cuddle, simply lying intertwined not moving, just listening to each other breathing, taking in their aromas, caressing each other, exploring their bodies together. Now, he couldn't get close to her even to touch her. She wouldn't go out choosing instead to spend her days in bed or curled up on the settee in the lounge endlessly flicking through the channels on the cable network. He knew something was wrong, but he did not know what it was or how to get her to talk to him. She had found it hard to open up to anyone not even her brother Tyrone, even though they were very close. It was Tyrone's idea that they sit her down and would not leave her unless she opened up to them and tell them what was troubling her.

Nelson recalled that night, Tyrone on one side of her he on the other. She was sobbing uncontrollably, shouting at them to leave her alone, get out of her room. Tyrone had told her that he was not going anywhere; he was there for the duration unless she opened up.

"You're my little sis and I hate seeing you like this, come on talk to me, I'm here for you, you get me"

She had managed to control herself, apart from a few involuntary sobs, she had looked at Nelson, her eyes were red and puffy, she looked like she had had an allergic reaction to something. Nelson noticed her eyes were wild and staring, almost begging Tyrone not to force her to speak. Tyrone simply held her tighter and whispered quietly into her ears, kissed her ears and continued to whisper. Nelson sat straight backed rigid fearing what it was that was troubling her, he knew it was nothing good and his mind raced through a hundred scenarios all as bad as each other. He felt helpless and he didn't like it, he wanted to click his fingers, hold her close, caress her, run his fingers through her hair, whisper sweet nothings into her ear, then everything will be alright and they could continue where they had left off all those weeks ago.

Nothing was going to make it alright, Nelson knew this the minute she began to speak, he trembled uncontrollably, first with fear, then he bristled with anger. The more she talked the angrier he got, he wanted to tell her to be quiet not to say anymore, that was enough he couldn't listen to anymore. It went through his mind, but he didn't want to say it but it came out anyway;

"Was it my fault?"

"Why do you think that it was your fault, how could you be to blame. I don't know, I just don't know, why me, what have I done to anyone, I don't deserve this!"

He felt a fool for blurting out, but he felt like a coward, he was unable to protect her and he had always thought that he could. She was his and he must protect her at all times. Tyrone had looked at him as if to say get a grip, it's not about you. Salisha carried on talking, each word churning him up inside, he couldn't look at her but could still see in his mind her lips moving, tears streaming down her face, the sudden uncontrollable sobs, the deep sighs and then he heard Tyrone crying. This whole situation was crazy, but he knew that they had to let her talk to let it out in order to start the healing process.

She started by talking about this cocky young boy outside school who had wolf whistled her and her friends, blowing kisses and calling to them. How he and two of his friends ran up to them and started talking to Miranda. One of them had grabbed her by the arm demanding a kiss and how the young one who had wolf whistled pulled him off and scolded him for not being a gentleman around ladies. He seemed pleasant enough and how that act had reminded her of Nelson, the kind of thing he would do, rescuing a damsel in distress. They talked for a little while, asked her what her name was, what she was studying, that sort of thing, he introduced himself. After that she saw him on a few other occasions outside school, they exchanged pleasantries and he was always nice, not like his friends who behaved like dogs on heat, pulling at any girl that walked past them. He wasn't handsome, but he wasn't ugly either. Dressed well, characterised by the fact that he was dripping in jewellery, two heavy chaps on each hand, three gold sovereign rings, three chunky chains round his neck, one with a gold marijuana leaf emblem, he looked like the archetypal villain, but he was so young.

There was a girl's thing at Miranda's house the next week, girls only. She had then looked at Nelson and asked him if he remembered it, remembered him wanting to go, but she had told him that he couldn't as it was girls only. It was something they did on a regular basis, just girls sitting around talking about boys, make up, clothes, sex, parents, girls venting their spleen safe in the knowledge that no boys were around.

Then there was a knock on the door and in walked those boys four of them, aged from about fifteen to nineteen. Miranda asked them to leave but they just pushed past her and made beelines towards them. She noticed the young courteous boy who made an immediate beeline for her. He wasn't pleasant anymore, grabbing her by the arm and telling her she was his, she was the one, he owned her. He was very strong and tried to push himself onto her; she had pushed him off and told him to behave himself.

"Me is Junior Shotta, an' when me want something me just tek it, scene!"

She described how he had pushed her into the adjoining dining room, how she tried to push past him and open the door, but the door wouldn't open someone or something was blocking it from the other side. Salisha had paused, sobbed louder than before, breathed heavily and sighed a deep mournful sigh, which caused both Nelson and Tyrone to jump up and look at her. She managed to straighten up and looked up at both of them. This made them sit back down by her side; Tyrone whispered again to her and kissed her on the forehead, offering her solace and comfort in order that she could carry on. Nelson just sat by her side arm around her shoulder smouldering, not wanting to hear what happened next, but wanting to hear hoping that it wasn't as bad as he had envisaged. Hoping that she would describe how she kicked him in the balls, slapped him hard, picked up a vase, an umbrella, a chair, anything smashing him over the head, pushing the door open and running out to freedom, but she didn't.

Salisha took a deep breathe then continued. She told them how she had pushed as hard as possible against the door, but it wouldn't budge. He came up behind her and pushed himself against her rubbing his penis against her buttocks, she recalled that he was aroused because he had an erection. She described how he pushed his hands underneath her arms and started to grope her breasts, then telling her how nice they felt.

"Girl, you have nice tings man, dem feel real good, you like it, huh, you like it don'cha'"

She could feel him undoing his trousers, one hand now feeling her buttocks and trying to pull down her trousers. She explained to Nelson that she was wearing the Top Shot culottes with the three inch belt they had bought when they had gone on one of their trips to the West End, asking him if he remembered them, remembered her trying them on and how he really liked them because they showed off her figure and looked really stylish all at the same time.

Nelson, felt useless he couldn't speak couldn't answer her all he could emit was a throaty croak like a bullfrog. He could feel the tears welling up in his eyes, he wanted to cry, in fact he wanted to wail and scream. His hands and fingers felt stiff and tingled, he looked at the wall if only he could get up he could relieve the feelings in his hands by pounding on the wall. He felt water trickle down his face, he wanted to wipe away the sweat and the tears but he could not move, he was mesmerised by her words, the sound of her voice, the sobbing all contrived to put him in a trance like state forcing him to listen.

She told how, in the same position he had forced her hand down to his erect penis, forced her to hold it, urging, ordering her to jerk him off, one hand still on her breast, the other holding her hand holding his erection. The other hand then trying to pull down her trousers, they wouldn't give the three inch belt holding firm against his urgings. He had then spun her around and tried to force her down onto her knees. Knowing what he wanted her to do she fought harder screamed, flailed her arms as best she could to fight him off and stay upright. At one point she staggered backwards hitting her head against the door, this made her feel dizzy. He had pounced on her pulling at her top, trying to force her down towards his manhood still erect. She described how she had braced her head and shoulders against the door and sprang forward knocking him off balance, how he grabbed at her getting a firm grip on her arm and pulled her forward both of them falling in a heap on the floor. How she had landed on top of him, felt his erection hard and wet on her exposed stomach. She managed to bite him on the shoulder, got her hands free and slapped him, once, twice three times she couldn't remember all she knew was that she was fighting for life.

Suddenly there was a loud bang on the door, a whistle a muffled shout;

"Shotta, come man, old bill are coming, I'm gone man, let's go..."

He pushed her off him and ran for the door, stumbling over his trousers normally hanging just below his hips now they were nearer to his knees, one hand holding them up the other groping for the door knob. He mumbled something to her and left. She described the sounds once he had ran from the room, during the attack she heard nothing except the rushing sound made by long grass in the wind, now she could hear all manner of sounds from her friends screaming, shouting, berating someone. Then a hush, silence, then whispered voices like a stagehand providing the actors with their lines as they stood on stage in front of an enraptured audience.

Miranda came in first, she looked like a witch, her eyeliner and mascara had run so much they were now just black splodges around her eyes, spiking where they had joined her tears and running down her face. Her hair was a mess as if it was blowing away in the wind, her top was torn. She had run to Salisha apologising every step of the way, they hugged, they cried, others joined them. In the aftermath, no one was hurt, apart form minor sexual assaults all were safe. One of them had pretended to call the police and the sound of sirens answering another emergency call had made them jittery and caused them to leave. The girls had given as good as they got and managed to fight them off, but couldn't get them away from the door to the dining room where she was.

Both Nelson and Tyrone gave out simultaneous sighs, but neither said a word. Salisha turned to Nelson and held him tightly, crying harder now she had let out what happened that night. Nelson held her just as tightly, he didn't want to let her go, he wanted to show her that he still cared. All the while anger was simmering inside him, he could hear it boiling up throughout him. His stomach was in knots, his head hurt, his throat was dry. He knew little Shotta or Everton, he also knew how connected he was, but that made no difference to him, he was going to get him. All he could think about was revenge on the cowardly little bastard.

Nelson had forgotten that Tyrone was there, but was shook into reality by Tyrone letting out a loud roar like a lion about to sink its teeth and claws into his prey. Tyrone sprung up from the bed his face distorted by rage. He began pacing up and down the room. He turned to Salisha and asked her, demanded from her if that was it that he didn't do anything else, why didn't she tell him before, good that she told him now, he'll make it right for her, he'll get that cowardly little bastard. He then looked at Nelson;

"Are you with me Bro? Everyone knows that little cunt, you with me in this? I know where he lives, where he hangs out, we'll get him on his own and see how he likes it, you with me Bro? Don't worry Sis, don't worry!"

Salisha tried to talk them out of it, but they couldn't back down, what would that make them if they were not seen to defend their sister, their girlfriend, family.

THE STAR CHAMBER Chapter 7

I had one of those days that all prosecutors dread, nothing seemed to go right. As usual I was in the Magistrates Court, it was going to be a very busy day, the lists were full and more were expected from custody at the police stations. The night before the administrators couldn't locate all the papers for the cases that were allocated to me, so for each case I had half the story or no story at all. On arriving at court I was informed that more were due from custody, it had been a busy weekend. The usual crap, shoplifters, wife beaters, addicts in possession, Vietnamese and Chinese for selling DVD's. Amongst these was Johnson Cole, what little papers I had confirmed that he had originally been arrested for the attempted murder of some young man.

The facts were sketchy but he had got into an argument with this guy who had apparently bumped into him at Florence's Nightclub in Clapton, the other guy had apologised, but Johnson wouldn't accept his apology saying the guy had disrespected him, pulled out a knife and as the guy was walking away stabbed him in the back. Unfortunately for the police they could find no witnesses who actually saw the incident, many had confirmed that the two had argued and that there was some kind of confrontation, but no one saw a knife or the actual stabbing. All they could do to hold him was to arrest him for resisting arrest and assaulting a police officer, then whilst in the cells, using foul and abusive language.

I had got through most of the list, the usual guilty pleas to taking a bottle of Jack Daniels, or slapping her a little bit, or it's for my own use and so on. The Magistrates seemed particularly lenient that day, none of them were given custody, most were put off for reports, or received fines and then given time to pay, £5 per week £10 per week. One guy even paid his £100 fine and £50 costs there and then waving a wad of £20 notes at the Magistrates and me, asking if we had change, the whole public gallery laughed and the cocky defence lawyer smirked and winked at me.

This defence lawyer was particularly conceited, who I had been up against many times. He was one for long speeches to the bench laden full of clichés about the hard life his client had and how he was trying to amend his ways, had signed onto a drug treatment course, was actively seeing care workers, how society dealt him bad cards but he was now bucking the trend and so on. The majority of these defendants were back in court within two weeks for exactly the same thing and he would trot out the same old sorry excuses. Worst of all the Magistrates would swallow it call for reports, adjourn the case then when they came back armed with the probations report would recommend some sort of community service order, or if they decided on prison give them the minimum sentence. This meant that with time served they'd be out within weeks.

I knew of the firm this particular defence lawyer worked for, they did not have a very good reputation amongst the fraternity. I had even been approached by one of their partners to work for them, they were on a particular aggressive recruitment drive and had approached most of the defence lawyers in the area to come work for them, as long as they had duty solicitor status, making vague promises of large salaries and even larger caseloads. Quite a few joined, but most had left again within a year, the working conditions not being conducive to a healthy lifestyle, working all night at police stations then back all day at court and still have a large caseload to run, without any administrative support. But this guy had worked there for about five years, so I suppose he had staying power.

I just didn't like him; it didn't make my mood any better when I learned that he was representing Johnson Cole. During the morning more papers arrived, delivered by an out of breath clerk, they were badly copied and not numbered properly. From reading the arresting officer's notebooks, Johnson had given them quite a time. He was abusive from the moment they had walked up to him, swearing at them, mocking them, the last straw was when he spat in their faces and laughed at them. Batons drawn, they beat him to the ground struggling to get handcuffs on him, they had him in a choke hold and almost broke his arms forcing them behind his back. He continued to struggle as four officers lifted him and threw him into the back of the van. At the station he carried on hurling abuse, so it was decided that he remained in cuffs. The officers' notebooks also noted the injuries they suffered, but remained silent regarding the injuries they had inflicted.

On his arrival at the police station, the cocky lawyer demanded that the handcuffs be removed and he managed to calm Johnson down. He went through the doctor's report outlining Johnson's injuries, noting that he was fit for interview. During the interview he managed to get the police to agree that they had no eye witness evidence or even a weapon linking his client to the attempted murder, not even the victim could positively identify Johnson;

"It was dark man, he was tall and skinny wearing a white shirt and he had a thick rope chain, that's all I remember, it happened so quickly, I turned my back and the bastard stabbed me, I'm sure it was him, had to be him, everyone knows his rep.."

After lengthy questioning, mainly about the assault the police dropped the allegation of attempted murder. There was no positive identification by the victim, knowing it was him and proving it was just too hard. No one could find the knife and when he was arrested he was wearing a yellow shirt and no necklace. From reading his list of previous offences, Johnson had certainly been a busy boy. He had various for assaults, street robberies, possession of drugs, supplying drugs, money laundering. He had done the lot, served lengthy periods in prison, where he simply honed his skills and became even nastier.

During the afternoon recess I had reason to go down to the cell area, I needed one of the arresting officers to verify part of his statement, he was in the cells talking with an old colleague. Before I got to him I had passed the holding area, where I noticed Johnson and the lawyer in a huddle going through his case, Johnson didn't seem happy, but that seemed to be his everyday demeanour.

"Look man, scene I ain't staying in dis place, bin ere all morning and me is fucked off now, dem fucking judges mus' let me out, scene"

"You will get bail they haven't anything apart from your abusive language, I can tell you the most you will get is a fine, I will make sure I will emphasise the injuries you sustained in an unprovoked attack by those officers. Now they will talk about the stabbing and that there was an intention to kill, but you mustn't say anything as they do not have anything on you regarding that incident."

"Cha man, dem is to stupid too get me on dat, course I stab up him raas, blood claat likkle bwoy come dis respec me..."

"Look shut up you can't say that, they haven't got anything, you'll be out this afternoon if you shut up, I promise you..."

"Bloodclaat bwoy, nex' time he will know I, should a kill his raas!"

"Shhh!"

I walked past them, I don't think they noticed me; they were too engrossed in ruling their own little worlds. It took all my resolve to walk past and not say anything, I was amazed at how cold and calculating this guy was and at the same time awestruck at his barefaced disregard for the law. But, he was right, he was going to get away with it and he was going to continue in the same way and he will definitely hurt someone again. Suppose it was Nelson next, or one of his friends, at that point I felt weak and inadequate. All my years of experience, the number of people I had ensured were locked up, I always thought that was all what was needed that the law, justice will prevail. But, this guy was living proof that we were not doing anything to make the streets safe, we were letting people like Johnson Cole back on the streets to do whatever they wanted. And he was going to be freed that afternoon.

In court I sat down whilst Johnson was dragged and pushed up from the cells to the defendant's cages. He had a cocky air and was berating the security guards for pushing and shoving him. He stood and gave out his name and smiled at me as they read out the charges, he smiled at the bench and in a loud voice shouted Guilty. I outlined the case against him and asked for the maximum sentence. His Lawyer then stood and began waxing lyrically about his clients hard upbringing, not knowing his father, a junkie mother, his complete contrition about this incident, how he felt slighted by the police suggestions that he had stabbed someone, how he'd been on various drug treatment and training orders (DTTO) which had not helped him, he was helping himself and he had a job. Someone actually employed this person. That was the clincher for the bench; they let him go with a £50 fine and a community service order. I could still hear Johnson laughing as he walked out of the courthouse. The arresting officers simply shrugged their shoulders resigned to the fact that he was back on the streets. I simply seethed knowing that there was nothing that I could do about it; I couldn't even raise the conversation I had overheard. His lawyer came to shake my hand I carried on shuffling my papers and ignored him.

Later that evening I met up with Jerry and Terry, went to our local. I was first to arrive so I ordered the drinks and got a table in a quiet part of the bar. I needed to talk to them about a plan I had, which had been on my mind for a while, and this Johnson Cole episode had launched it back to the front of my mind. All afternoon I had been thinking about it, fine tuning it, going back over it, fine tuning it some more. Listing in my head the pro's and con's, thinking about various scenarios. Would it work? What did I want from it? Would Jerry and Terry go for it? Whilst I waited for them I went through it again, I had wanted to write it down but became paranoid that someone would find it, read it, and then it was all up before we had even started, so I kept it all in my head. I rehearsed it, pro's and con's, reasons, how, where, when and why.

Terry was first to arrive, he was quiet, seemed a bit distant. I asked him what seemed to be the matter; it wasn't like him to be so pensive. He explained that he had heard some bad news, one of his boys was killed yesterday, he was on his own hanging out around his estate talking to his girlfriend on the phone when someone just shot him and stole his phone.

"It's just mad out there man, if they wanted his phone they should have just taken it and walked away. I can't fathom a reason why they would shoot him and leave him for dead. This kid had mended his ways he had gone back to college, his girlfriend had just had a baby, he was turning his life around. These bastards have no morals, they must be empty inside. I don't think I can do this anymore man, I feel lost!"

Just then Jerry walked in and sidled into his chair, he looked from me then to Terry and just frowned. He looked like he had the worries of the world on his shoulders as well. Terry repeated what he had just told me, Jerry looked at him and frowned, then sighed.

"Yeah, I knew the guy as well he had just started hanging out with Nelson, he's been round to my place a couple of times. He was a funny, sincere kid, had his eyes open knew what he wanted, it's a damn shame man, someone has got to do something about this, it's like we're under siege. Something, a gesture, some action otherwise our whole community is just going to implode, listen I'm there with anyone who wants to do anything!"

I described my day, went through the trauma of coming up against Johnson Cole, told them how I felt knowing he did this and simply walked out of the court without not even a slapped wrist. I said to them that for all we knew it was him who had stabbed their guy that, if anything was going to be done he has got to be on the list. They had asked me why I couldn't do anything, I explained the problems to them, how there wasn't enough evidence, even though everyone was sure it was him and even after I had heard his 'confession' I shouldn't have been there shouldn't have been listening, it was all to do with hearsay, him and his lawyer would simply deny it and I would be hauled up so I had to let it pass. I explained how it felt for me and I looked at both of them. I asked them if they were serious when they said that they wanted to do something about this, get involved, make a difference, be part of change in the neighbourhood.

Jerry looked at me and simply nodded his head. Terry didn't look up but said;

"I'm fed up of talking we need action, we need to protect our people!"

This was my cue to go through my plan. I asked them first if they had ever seen the film 'Star Chamber' where Michael Douglas played a superior court judge joins a group of other Lawyers and police fed up with villains getting away on technicalities or insufficient evidence form a secret society who deliberated on their cases and mete out their own form of justice.

I told them that I think that if they wanted action this was it. We form our own Star Chamber, all three of us, and we go after these murderers, villains, recidivists, whatever you want to call them. We put the fear of God into them make them think about what they are doing, drive them out of the communities or ensure that they come to their senses. It's not going to be easy; the first thing is that no-one must know that it is us. We'll need a van a transit van would be good, we could line it and stuff so you can't hear the noise from outside, and then we'll need somewhere to take them to 'persuade' them. To 'persuade' them anything goes. We could wear overalls, baseball caps and the Zorro masks I picked up from a fancy dress shop.

Both Terry and Jerry laughed as they tried on the masks. Jerry said that he had some job lot overalls at work and mentioned some designer name; I suppose if we are going to do this thing then we'd look good doing it. Terry said that the mechanics next door to the centre had an old white transit they occasionally used to pick up heavy loads, he had used it occasionally for the Centre and that they had given him a spare set of keys just in case he needed the van and they were busy.

I took it from their response that they were in, the only problem we had was where to take them without drawing attention to ourselves. Jerry and I went through various places, but none seemed appropriate some problem with the location always came up. Terry was quiet and thoughtful so I gave him a nudge;

"Okay, I think Alton Weekes might be able to help us out, you've both heard of the Torture Chamber, well we could use that."

I nearly choked on my drink and Jerry fell off his chair. We had both thought that the Torture Chamber was a myth, but here we are Terry confirming that it wasn't urban legend but a real place. He told us where it was, it was out in the middle of nowhere, no-one went there at night much less during the day unless they had business in one of the other lock ups, it sounded perfect. The only problem was that we would have to involve Alton Weekes. Terry told us that Alton would not be a problem, that after the death of his little brother he would probably want to join us.

Jerry smiled and looked at Terry who now had a big grin on his face, shook his head and said to him;

"Listen, wait man I thought you were the saviour of these kids, that talking to them offering them something else besides violence and drugs was the way, look at you man you're salivating at the thought of getting your hands on these guys!"

"Listen bro, you must understand, I still strongly believe that and I will continue to help anyone who wants to be helped, but there are some monsters out there who ain't gonna respond to that, they only know violence that is the only way they will take it seriously. I still believe that I will be doing some good."

"Listen what about you lawyer man, aren't you fighting the fight in the courtroom, don't you think that doing something like this is a juxtaposition between what you do now and you meting out your own justice?"

Terry and I smiled looking at each other and both said 'Juxtaposition'? At the same time. Jerry explained what he meant.

"Listen, two ideas so contrary to each other but nevertheless running side by side."

He was right, I think we were all in that state we had our day jobs where we either defended the people, or fought for justice, or simply wanted to protect our own. Then we are presented with an insurmountable problem, which impelled us to act and those actions would be against what we had thus far considered, but we held onto the belief that our actions were for redemption not retribution as long as we held onto that then we would be right. I had felt strange as I talked about the Star Chamber and what I had thought up; somehow I imagined how Eldridge Cleaver and the other members of the Black Panther party for self defence felt arming themselves against the state to demand their rights as written in the constitution. They had right on their side and so do we, but this was juxtaposed by the very fact that what we were intending to do was legally wrong.

I outlined how Terry and I were best placed to identify those for the Star Chamber treatment, Johnson Cole being the first as I had enough information about him in my case, where he lives, where he hangs out. We had to decide how we were going to do this, but first Terry had to speak to Alton Weekes about using the torture chamber. I had resolved to keep an eye on Cole looking for times when he was alone in readiness for our action.

Jerry had asked what about our voices most of these guys know our voices, Terry through his community work, me through my court work and him because he was simply a star. Terry hit on a good idea and explained how we could stuff cotton wool into our mouths puffing out our cheeks this would give our voices a muffled sound and would be harder to detect, especially if we talk with accents. We all agreed on this, we had then racked our brains for any other little thing but felt happy that we had covered everything.

I think we all felt and believed that we were going to be the vanguard to save our communities, people finally doing something to rid the streets of fear, the phalanx marching unstoppable through the hordes of street gangsters. I also felt enlightened, I had feared that either Terry or Jerry or both of them would dismiss my idea, tell me I was a fool and that I shouldn't think like that. But, they both had had their fill seeing another young life wiped out for the price of a phone, or another young girl ripped of her innocence, had profoundly affected them. They saw a different aftermath to me, I saw it in the courthouse when someone had been caught, witnessed first hand the process that decided if they were innocent or guilty and then societies retribution. On the other hand Terry and Jerry saw the affect the loss had on the families and the communities. They felt the increasing fear in the air as another young body is laid to rest or another girl's virginity is burned away. They saw the scars, the blemishes, the bruises of yet another unprovoked attack, and they knew every cut, every slash, every bullet was another nail in the coffin of the community.

Now we felt that we could do something about it, something tangible and real, which would have a real and everlasting affect. Something we hoped would affect change and save the community from the minority that was tearing it apart. We weren't vigilantes, we didn't run around in a mob burning tyres and running amok. We saw ourselves as heroes, saviours of our communities, protectors of our families. I went home that night feeling high, higher than I felt for a long while. I couldn't sleep, ideas running through my head. The faces of the lost souls we were going to save flashing through my mind, no longer full of hubris. We were on the threshold of something big and it did excite me, I couldn't wait to get started.

Terry had said that he would speak to Alton Weekes in the morning assuring us there would be no problems. Jerry promised to have the overalls ready for when we would start. Everything was set for go.

JOHNSON COLE chapter 8

The next day court whizzed by, I had quite a few successes, it seemed like my new found confidence had rubbed off on the benches who sided with me more than usual. The paperwork was in good order, arresting officers urbane and good natured. In the afternoon I noticed a name on the list Johnson Cole, I searched out the papers and read the charges, street robbery, he had held up two fourteen year old girls on a bus on their way home from school. Took their mobiles, their money and their Oyster cards. Then for good measure groped them, probably would have gone further but he was on a bus and people started to get on. Victim statements said that he strolled off the bus whistling a Dizzy Rascal tune.

I was not the prosecutor on this one, but as I had finished my caseload I sat in the back of the gallery my gaze fixed on Johnson. I took in his every mannerism, the way he stood, how he cocked his head every time his name was mentioned, his smirk when asked how he would plead;

"Not guilty man, mistaken identity John Bull always picking on me..."

I watched how he laughed, flashing his gold incisor. I noted it all but unlike the day before I smiled I had his number and I was onto him. I didn't even blink when he was released on bail and a trial date was set. It felt like I owned him, his life was in my hands he had to change his ways or feel the force of the Star Chamber but he just didn't know it yet.

I had outlined to Terry and Jerry that it wasn't our aim to kill anyone not like in the original. We were 'persuaders', we were going to convince these people, the low life that they are going to change their ways and fall into line with the rest of the community, that the community had had enough of their fighting, thieving and debauchery and was fighting back. If they didn't want to see us again then simple, behave. If they carried on with their criminal ways we will visit them again. I had rehearsed the speech by Jules in 'Pulp fiction' and re-read my bible to get it right; Ezekiel 25:17.

"The path of the righteous man is beset on all sides by the inequities of the selfish and the tyranny of evil men. Blessed is he who in the name of charity and goodwill shepherds the weak through the valley of darkness, for he is truly his brother's keeper and the finder of lost children. And I will strike down upon thee with great vengeance and furious anger those who attempt to poison and destroy my brothers. And you will know my name is the Lord when I lay my vengeance upon thee."

I explained that this was to be our rallying cry that it summed up exactly, precisely what it was that we were doing. We were carrying out good work and were crusaders for right, for peace and for our brethren against those who had lost their way and were now poison and were certainly destroying our brothers. Sitting at the back of that courtroom I wanted to look Cole in the eye and recite it to him word for word and with the same force, so that he knew what was about to befall him, give him an insight into his fate. But, I simply smiled as our eyes met, he sneered at me remembering our encounter the previous day and mouthed the word motherfucker to me, I smiled and gave him the thumbs up sign and left the courtroom. I couldn't wait to meet up with Terry in the evening anxious for news of the torture chamber, I had this guy in my sights and I wasn't going to let him go.

I had given myself the job of scout, because of my position I was able to obtain information on likely targets. Everyday I received papers, statements, antecedents giving their names, age, height, eye colour, known hang outs, associates and their crimes. It was easy for me to compile any dossier I wanted on these miscreants, in fact, it was everyday reading for me no-one would suspect. I just had to be smart and not leave a paper trail that could lead back to us. I had no fear of the police; the care I had to take was that we were not found out by any of our intended victims, which would be dangerous for us and our families.

I started to take more of an interest in the people in court and what they were charged with. I made a mental note of their demeanour, how they behaved, how they dressed and how they spoke. I watched them huddled in corners with their solicitor or barrister, anxiously shuffling paper and making scribbled notes, underlining, scoring out, preparing their defences. I saw the first timers, not used to the process, looking worried, asking what will happen to them. I saw the recidivists, they were doing all the talking, asking how they can plea it down, asking about the evidence, telling their lawyer that they ain't doing 'bird'. I watch those paying fines, wads of cash flashed a fiver, a tenner rolled off, the wad back into their pockets, then listened to them plead poverty, ask for more time to pay, gold watch flashing in the fluorescent light. I watched the lines of people standing outside having a quick smoke before they were called on, laughing about their misdemeanour, or other antics they had been up to.

Down in the cells I saw the ones held in custody and produced for court looking dishevelled, gasping for a fag or a drink or both, names written in chalk outside their cell ready to wipe off as soon as they were gone. I saw the victims sitting on benches outside the courtroom, anxiously waiting to give evidence if called, being ignored by my colleagues the prosecution. All manner of life in one place, one building, all waiting for justice to be meted out, for them to feel the full force of blind justice, but justice that is measured and sure and those handing out justice to feel the power as they deliver the sentence and issue those harsh words, 'GUILTY' then more harsh words, fine, suspended sentence, community service order or how about drug and rehabilitation order. Then as they leave court the smile, the laugh, with disdain and disrespect to blind justice; unable to see this right in front of her very nose.

Johnson was every bit a part of this, he understood it all, been there in front of a bench many times. He walked around the court with an indolent air, nothing could touch him. He had played the same cards and had always come up trumps. His past always there for him to play on whenever he needed it. Mother an addict, never knew his father, 'uncles' coming and going, beating up his mother, and him. Drugs and violence was all he knew, but he had a social worker, he kept his appointments with probation, turned up for his 'rehabilitation'. Always relapsed, but is it any wonder the life he had to endure. All the while he was laughing at them, he had no intention of rehabilitating, he enjoyed his life, and he enjoyed hurting people. If someone had something he wanted all he had to do was take it. It wasn't stealing to him, he just wanted it and there it was. He enjoyed taking drugs, the odd smoke, but he had moved on from 'weed' crack was where it was at, gave him a better buzz, lasted longer. So if he had to steal from those who were too weak to protect themselves in order for him to fund his habit so be it. Every time he sucked on his pipe he said a thank you to his last victim.

He had tried working, had many jobs from working in kitchens, serving hamburgers, pot man in a pub, street cleansing, gutting chickens, but there were too many rules, too many people wanting to give him orders, had to get up early, which he could never do as he was still high from the night before. Those people he worked with and who became his latest victims, rather than get a pay packet from them they were his next trick in order to score. The ones he despised the most would feel the most pain as he held them up and ripped them of their possessions. As he saw it, why should he work, scrimp and save like all the other rats around when he could take what he wanted, and if he got caught he always had old reliable excuses to get him off and back on the streets. He had no time for the community, couldn't care less what people thought of him. He saw it as he was brought into this world alone and he will leave it the same way, he didn't need to care about anyone as no-one cared about him. All he cared about was when he was going to get his next hit.

I watched him as he left court, no sooner had he left the courtroom he got into an altercation with someone. Caused quite a commotion, security was there separating him from the other youth, who was swearing and shouting at him. It appears that as Johnson was walking towards the exit rather than walk around people he decided to walk through barging and pushing his way through. This one guy took exception and pushed him back, Johnson must have threatened him and shoved him hard, which is when his friends intervened, at the same time as security. Johnson was ushered out of the court and then stood looking back into the court standing tall he raised his hand in the motion of a gun and motioned as if he was shooting at everyone then he was gone, presumably to get his long awaited hit.

Ezekiel kept going through my mind as I watch him amble down the High Street "*And I will strike down upon thee with great vengeance and furious anger those who attempt to poison and destroy my brothers. And you will know my name is the Lord when I lay my vengeance upon thee.*" Back at the office I took notes of his address and normal hang outs in order to plan our move on him. He normally hung out at a known Crack house on Livingstone Road; he lived in a flat in the tower block at the end of this road. If he wasn't there he could be found walking around the High Street normally with a can of strong lager or Cider in his hand haranguing anyone who got in his way. From there if he had some money he would be in the Shooting Star public house playing pool and hustling cigarettes and more drinks. He certainly was a creature of habit; I knew that it would be easy to find him whatever the time.

Life seemed so simple for him; wake up, drugs, drink, and some food probably. Have a nap, more drugs, drink, pester someone, count the money in his pocket, if not enough he simply had to find a target and rob them. Drugs, drink, sleep. On the rare occasion the drugs hadn't sapped his libido, find a crack bitch, get her high and have sex, take some more drugs to take away the taste of the crack bitch, then take some more as sex never measured up to sucking up that wonderful smoke, nothing like a chemical high!

I was eager to find out if Terry had spoken with Alton Weekes and rather than await his phone call I decided as soon as I had finished work that I would go to his office, better we talk face to face than have ears pricked listening to our phone conversation. When I arrived at Terry's he greeted me with a smile and a nod, which I took to mean that we were on.

Terry explained what happened when he contacted Alton Weekes, he had gone to Alton's office they had started by talking about Everton and how his death had affected his whole family. Alton had told him that his little brother was out of control and that his violent demise was inevitable, which was why he was desperate that Terry try and turn him away from the gangster life. He said that he wasn't surprised by what he had heard from the streets about what he had been getting up to and that because of this had come to terms with his death. In a funny sort of way he did not have any malice for his killers, but remained frustrated that no one seemed to know who had done it. He told Terry how he had been warned off by the police, which is why he had to play it cool, but that he was still searching for them and had to do something once the heat was off him. Terry seemed to think that he knew who it was but was just biding his time.

He had told Alton what it was that we wanted to do, he thought it was best just to lay it down straight and fast. If Alton wasn't in on it or thought we were being stupid he simply had to walk away and nothing more would be said, but he listened intently. Terry outlined to him the type of person we wanted to 'tame' and why. He also stressed that we were not out to kill anyone just put them back on track encourage them to become good citizens in the only language that they seemed to understand – FORCE.

Terry explained to him that we were not Knights in shining armour or that we wanted to change the world, just that we were sick and tired of these characters scaring the whole community forcing more and more people to bear arms to protect themselves, of our kids, our wives and mothers being scared to go out scared to confront someone for fear of violence. We were sick and tired of being scared to act like good citizens and confront misbehaviour, in case we became victims. It was time someone in the community fought back and made these miscreants scared to misbehave, make them look over their shoulders or think twice before they did some despicable act to someone in our family.

Terry had spoken at length but he did not get anything back from Alton, who just sat listening intently. So he carried on and went on to explain about how he saw it every day a new mini gangster in the making wanting to be the new Junior Shotta. Terry told him that he did not think that Alton would want that to be his brother's legacy and that his memory could be part of the solution rather than just another springboard to more misery for a mother somewhere.

"You know I see it every day, someone trying to be a big shot, I see their victims, I try to turn them away from that life see the bigger picture. I then have to console their victims. I see mothers every day and I wonder if they are going to be the next parent who loses someone to some act of mindless violence. It's inevitable that one of them is going to lose someone, I try to make it not happen tomorrow, to prolong the hope that it will not happen to them, but you know I feel useless, I feel like I'm just treading water. I need to do something else, something more drastic. You might think me stupid, and it is a bit stupid what we are planning, but it feels to me that it is all we have left, are you with us?"

He could see Alton thinking about it, he had nodded along with what Terry had to say, had smiled and frowned in equal measure. Finally he spoke and told Terry that the chamber was his to use as long as it did not get back to him.

"You know, maybe you've got a point. Everton was a fool but he was my brother, maybe we could do something for each other. I couldn't handle how it had affected my mother and even though I'm a bad man a settled community has got to be good for business. If you guys pull this off..."

The plan agreed with Alton was that we let him know when we wanted to use the Chamber, in case he had use of it, a kind of courtesy. He would make sure that none of his people would be around so that we had easy access; we just had to ensure that nothing got back to him or his organization.

We had the green light, it was all systems go and Johnson Cole was to be our first client. We called Jerry and set up a meeting so that we could plan when and how we were going to get Johnson Cole.

Jerry arrived carrying a box and showed us the overalls, Black with white stripes on the arms, we each took one. I was eager to try mine on; I had purchased the masks and passed them round. Jerry then pulled out a red, gold and green hat with hair extensions sewn in, like the Rasta hats you can buy from the tourist gift shops in Jamaica.

"Listen man, I've always wanted an excuse to wear it!"

He had put it on, both Terry and I fell off our chairs laughing, he looked anything but a Rasta man, but it was a good disguise and unless you knew him you would not think that it was Jerry. All we needed now was for him to get the accent right. This was difficult for him, he sounded more like Jim Davidson trying to sound Jamaican whilst telling his chalky jokes, pitiful, but he should get by, especially for what we had planned.

I started to describe Johnson Cole to the others, what he had been up to, the stabbings, the sex attacks, his general demeanour, his hang outs *et al*. I explained the legal position as to why he keeps walking out to terrorise more people. The fact that he was the product of a druggie mother, no father around to steer the ship, various uncles just wanting his mother, doing anything to get him out of the way. About him an indolent, disrespectful, drug ravaged bastard who didn't care about anyone or anything apart from himself. He needed our 'little persuasion' to be part of this community nothing else had worked, he had played the system, maybe we will have more luck.

Jerry was seething, but remained quiet, I kept looking at him, his eyes were smouldering red hot a sure sign that he was about to explode, I tried to stall it for as long as possible as I wanted to get everything straight about Johnson first. As soon as I had finished Jerry slammed the table with both fists and grunted he then let rip.

"Listen, you know, its people like this guy I see them all the time taking all of us for fools. If he wanted to change he could've but he didn't want to. Listen, that shit you were talking about no Father to steer the ship how many others have done okay without a Father, his mother keeps putting all that crap into her body then selling her body so she could get more of it into her, looks to me she is getting messed up all ways. And him yeah, listen, he's had social workers around him all his life rather than learn to live right he learns how to fuck the system and fool them, they give in to him too much and here is the product a shit on the streets fucking with us and mocking us. Now he's grown they leave him out there and we have to face the consequence, listen let's fuck this brother up, the sooner the better!"

I then described a usual day for Mr Cole, the Crack house, the pub, his walks up and down the High Road. I explained that by seven each evening he would be in or outside 'The Shooting Star' pub, if he wasn't there then he'd be somewhere around the High Road causing some sort of mischief or hassle. It would be easy to face up to him as he would either be drunk or drugged up or both, confront him and get him into the van, from there he's ours to do with what we want. I explained that our best bet was to get him away from the pub and too many seeing eyes. The pub is on a corner with an alley running behind it, my guess about Johnson was that he would be too lazy to use the toilet inside the pub and will use the alley to relieve himself. We will park the van adjacent to the alley and wait for him. If he doesn't use the alley he will be off on one of his strolls to cause some trouble, then we can choose where we get him, anywhere down the High Road. We will have to be quick, silence him quickly and get him into the van.

I told Terry that he needed to stay at the wheel in case we needed a quick getaway, but otherwise we would drive off nice and easy. So that meant Jerry and I would do the nabbing, just grab him silence him and straight into the van. Once in the van we must tie him up or restrain him in some way. I had this wire flex and old sack from work, which were strong enough so that he would not be able to break out. As soon as we jump out of the van the sack is over his head, get him from behind and throw him into the van. Jerry was to sit on his legs and I would tether him like a goat in a yard in Jamaica.

Terry explained that he had to square things with Weekesy first, so it will have to be tomorrow. He also explained that the van was being serviced today so it should be running okay by tomorrow as well.

"Is it just me or is everybody else nervous?"

The day went slowly, I could not concentrate on my work, luckily for me I had already cleared the decks to spend the day in the office preparing for a trial I had coming up. I had managed to evade the list officer who was looking for more Advocates to attend court for the new and overnight cases, this was my day in the office, my first one in months. I needed to clear my head in readiness for the night ahead and getting my head stuck in a pile of paperwork seemed to me to be the best idea. But, it wasn't, it was a bad idea, I just couldn't concentrate. The words on the documents seemed to gel into one I couldn't make them out for all I could tell I was reading Sanskrit. To make matters worse I spilt my tea over the unused information, if the defence ever called for it all they would be able to make out is whether I was drinking Earl Grey, Darjeeling or Sainsbury's best.

My mind kept going over the plan for tonight and each and every time we messed up, Jerry froze and Cole barged him out of the way, pulled a razor from his pocket and slashed me across the throat, whilst I lay bleeding on the floor Terry drove off with a loud screeching of tyres leaving Jerry and I to be sliced up into little pieces by a now eight foot tall Cole. Another scene played in my mind: just as things were going well, we had cased him thrown the sack over him, I had hold of him, then the sack rips open, Cole has now taken on the persona of the Incredible Hulk, as I hold him he continues to grow, I end up wrapped around one of his legs as he bounds along the High Road, at the same time Jerry grabs hold of his waist and both of us are pulled along in his slipstream neither us wanting, daring to let go as he is running so fast. We hear the van driven by Terry beeping behind us, but he cannot keep up, Jerry is the first to let go I look back and see him rolling and bouncing down the road body parts being ripped from his torso, I close my eyes and await the inevitable.

Whilst trying to dry out the tea stains I go over and over the plan, we park up, Jerry stands watch outside the pub, he signals us and we watch which direction he goes, hopefully he goes to the alley to relieve himself, once he's done we pounce so quickly we have him tethered and in the van before he knows what hit him. Alternatively, he walks off down the High Road, two junctions up there is a natural bend in the road visibility is not so defined, the van stops ahead of him just after the bend as he approaches Jerry and I jump out , etc, Surely nothing could go wrong.

Catching up with Jerry and Terry later on they seemed to have had very similar days to me. Terry had decided to attend a group meeting, with all the other Youth Development workers in the borough thinking that a nice boring meeting would get his mind off the forthcoming event. However, he was wrong he told me how the day had dragged on that it seemed to him the more they talked the slower time went, he had even convinced himself that time had actually stopped. There was one particular person at the meeting who had a very low droning voice that had a soporific effect if listened to for too long, who seemed to speak the most. Terry was sure he had fallen asleep for, at least, fifteen minutes, when he woke because of some weird hacking cough he looked at his watch, only thirty seconds had past and the bore was still speaking and the cougher was getting more guttural every second. He knew he had to get out of there so made up an excuse, after he received a fortunate text message, about trouble at the centre and them needing him there right away.

Jerry was more fortunate as he had a clear day free from any meetings or clients and spent the day quietly at home. He told me later that he spent most of the day perfecting his 'bad boy' voice, looking in the mirror with the Rasta hat on and trying his best "Harder they come" accent. He also showed me the 'walk' he had perfected a sort of limp but with a bounce at the last minute.

"Listen man, got to look and sound the part!"

The plan was that Terry would speak with Alton Weekes the night before; he confirmed the go ahead to use the 'Torture Chamber'. Terry would then pick up the van at six o'clock and pick us up at Jerry's place. Alton should by then have dropped off the keys and warned his people away from the garages. On picking us up we would drive to the 'Torture Chamber' to have a good look over the place and then go over the plan for the last time. At Seven O'clock we would set off on our pursuit of our prey.

The Torture Chamber was everything we thought that it would be, as we walked in Terry turned on the lights, which were located on a panel about one metre from the door, it was dark and dingy, the smell of damp and wet rot filled the air like an aerosol of testosterone. The sound of water could be heard running down one corner of it. In another corner was a large table with a large lamp taking up most of one corner. Laid out on the table under the lamplight was an array of tools, some I had never seen before, laid out sorted by size with the smallest being the furthest away from the lamp. In the middle of the room hanging from the ceiling was a set of chains which jangled and chimed as we opened the door. In between the chains hung a long flex and from this was one bulb light dangling menacingly over a small table and chair. The chair had remnants of rope attached to the back and the legs, if you looked closely you could see that this rope had smearing of dried blood. Blood could also be seen under the small table in the middle of the room and you could make out splattering of blood on the wall nearest to the door. Once you are in there is no escape unless you are released!

Jerry was fascinated with the 'tool table' staring wide eyed at the array of tools and implements, picking some up and swinging them in overhand, underhand, jabbing, uppercut motions, feeling out which one he liked the best, knowing that he was going to be using them soon. Terry and I watched him fascinated at how many uses he could get out of a wrench, without a nut or bolt in sight. We carried on talking, going over the plan making sure he knew when and where we would hit him depending on what his actions were. We had to call jerry three times, very loudly so engrossed he was in trying out the tools. We changed into our uniforms and readied ourselves to leave, at the doorway taking one more look, knowing that very soon we'd be back and at work.

Outside it had got dark, the area was dimly lit the whole estate was deserted the only noise being the sound of distant traffic on the motorway a few hundred metres away. We got in the van and set off for the High Road and the Shooting Star public house. Terry parked up in the side road behind the pub adjacent to the alley; locally known as 'Piss-head Alley' the smell told you why it was called that. I got out of the van putting on my flat cap, which managed to partially hide some of my face, zipped up my overall and walked around to the front of the pub to see if I could see our prey. There was a group of five young men milled around the front of the pub smoking, and talking loudly, each time a girl or women walked past they would wolf whistle and cat call, nothing very imaginative, but funny all the same, "Hey sweet biscuit!" being the best effort. I felt like David Attenborough on a Socio-anthropological expedition to view the natives in their natural habitat. I could not see the prey I thought that maybe he would be inside, so I tried to take a peek through the wags blocking the doorway, I couldn't make him out, maybe he had already set off down the High Road or was still getting high in the crack house. Then just as I was going to do an about turn I felt a shove in my back and heard a menacing voice;

"Move out me way geezer!"

It was him, he sauntered past me and through the wags at the doorway they opened up to let him through lest they get the same treatment as me. He nodded to them in a mock kind of respect, they nodded back, but it didn't look like they liked or respected him. I heard one of them call him a "Pussy" and another saying "quiet man you know he's always tooled up" "yeah, and he don't mind using it either!"

I went back to the van and told Terry and Jerry that he was there and all we needed now to do was to wait. Terry had found an R 'n' B station on the radio which was pumping out some old standards from old school days, we sat and waited nodding our heads and singing along to the music. A saxophone solo came on and we all imagined ourselves as Grover Washington Jr playing live at the Bijou. We were so engrossed we did not notice until it was too late our prey approach us to go down the alley. Jerry nudged me saying "is dat him?" I nodded. He looked directly into the van but his eyes seemed misted over he was clearly the worse for wear through either drink or drugs or both, so continued on his mission to find his favourite spot to relieve himself. Terry turned on the engine and moved the van so it was covering the alleyway. Jerry and I got out, went to the back of the van, opened the back doors and pretended we were mulling over something inside the van and waited for him to re-appear. It seemed like an eternity; Jerry exclaimed that that must be some record for pissing. Jerry had the sack in his hand I had the tape and the flex.

Finally, he re-appeared, he was muttering to himself about something and looking down at his shoes and trousers, even from where I was standing and looking out from the corners of my eyes I could see that he had pissed all over his trousers and shoes. He walked another two steps, Jerry and I were ready to pounce, when he stopped to inspect himself again and pulled from his sock what looked like a spliff, stand up and take a lighter from his pocket and proceeded to light the spliff, smiling when the flame took. He continued to walk with a self satisfied grin on his face. As he got up to the van Jerry let out a wail like a banshee and rushed over to him throwing the sack over his head. I ran over and threw the flex around his midriff and grabbed him around his chest, Jerry scooped up his legs and we threw him struggling into the back of the Van. I jumped in first and sat on him pulling on the flex and wrapping the tape around him and the sack. Jerry, before entering the van took quick glimpses up and down the road, no one was looking, no one saw. We banged on the back of the van and Terry took off, success we had our prey.

He didn't put up much of a fight, he struggled for a while, swore like a trooper, tried to sit up, swore again then he lay still breathing heavily and every now and again we would hear a sob. All the while Jerry was whispering to him telling him how we were going to break every finger, cut off his balls and shove them into his mouth that this was his last day on earth and he should start praying. This Jerry, I did not recognise, but I must admit that the events up to now gave me a high I had never felt before. It felt like I was on top of the world, nothing could stop me, I even remember thinking that it was better than sex, could it really be?

We could hear Terry singing at the top of his voice, the radio blaring out yet more rare groove old school music. He was driving well within the speed limit obviously it would be a bit awkward if we were stopped by police now, a youth and community leader, a prosecution lawyer and a company executive dressed in disguises and holding down a man tied up in a sack. I imagined the conversation would go something like this:

"Evening all, now what have we here then, would you mind explaining what he is doing in the back of your van?"

"Well, you see Officer he suffers from migraine and this is the only way for him to get over it?"

"You're nicked guys!"

It wasn't long before we had pulled up outside the Torture Chamber, Terry turned off the lights then turned off the engine, all was quiet except for Johnson heavy breathing and sobs. Jerry and I waited for the back doors to open then pushed him out of the van and lifted him into the chamber, then we put on our masks and gloves. We shoved him down into the chair in the centre of the chamber, Terry and I stood either side of him, Jerry had strolled over to the 'tool table' and was whistling one of the rare groove tunes as he started to select his favourite tools.

It was time to take the sack off him we both readied ourselves in case he tried to run or attack us. I untied the rope and pulled off the tape then I pulled the sack from over his head. He looked straight ahead blinking in the light beaming down on him from above his head, he then looked at Terry then at me, we were blocking his view of Jerry but he could certainly hear him whistling and hear the clanking of the tools being selected and de-selected by him. Neither Terry nor I spoke as I then tied his hands to the back of the chair. That was when I realised that the chair was actually screwed down into the floor, in order to move it you had to smash it, by the time you had done that you would have been restrained again, ingenious, they thought of everything.

He sat there with wild eyes staring from Terry, to me, to the door, he tried to look behind him too see what Jerry was doing. He looked up hearing the clanking and chiming of the chains, saw the heavy chains and sighed a deep sigh, which sounded like his soul leaving his body. He was ashen faced only his eyes were bright. He couldn't talk his eyes did the talking for him, pleading with us to let him go, have mercy on him. I can imagine that through his mind ran the thought, "I could do with a hit right now!"

We didn't speak for a while choosing to let him stew in the heady atmosphere that we had created. Jerry joined us and stood at the other side of the small table immediately opposite him. Without saying a word he dropped with a loud clang three selected tools onto the table, reached over and slapped him hard around the face. Terry and I looked from Jerry, to Johnson then at the tools. One was an oversized pipe wrench, the other was a large, fearsome looking spanner, I couldn't name the third tool. Again it was large and had a bulb shaped head with a wire stretching down to the base, it looked very heavy. I could see tears streaming down his face and a spot of blood in the corner of his mouth where Jerry had caught him with the slap.

Terry then reached over and slapped him hard on the other side of his face, seeing this I slapped him across the back of his head. We continued this treatment for about three minutes. His whole body was now trembling, I couldn't tell if he was still crying as both tears and sweat had combined to soak his face. We had him where we wanted him and it felt good, we wanted him scared of us, and he was, we wanted to get our message home. Terry was the first to speak, he put on his deepest, darkest voice and leant down so that his mouth was directly in line with Johnson's ear, as he spoke the tension in the air rose a further notch.

"We nah want to kill you, but we raas will if you don't listen and take heed to what we saying to you, you get me?" Then he slapped him again just to reinforce the message.

"We been watching you an' we nah like de way you carry on, you gwan like you is top a top when you is nuttin'. You like to use knife and you like to 'stress up women, you like to fuck up people for nuttin more than being next to you. How you like it, huh?" Another slap.

Jerry joined in raising up the large spanner and waving it menacingly right in front of Johnson's eyes.

"You want this, you listening to us, I should bash you aroun' de head and give you a lick for everyone you been troubling and fucking up. Listen, it's shits like you dat make people fraid to go out an we don't want people like you on we streets, it's time you tek dat in and mek you mind up!" He swung the spanner narrowly missing Johnson but making a loud thudding noise on the table.

Jerry looked at me and said, "why we don't just fuck him up now, he ain't tekking it in, soon as we let him go he back to his old ways, we should fuck him up now and be done wid it!"

I looked at Johnson and grabbed his chin, I turned his head towards me, I could see the fear in his eyes and I could smell it emanating from his every pore, we had him. I spoke to him in measured tones trying as much as possible to sound like Jules in "Pulp Fiction".

"The path of the righteous man is beset on all sides by the inequities of the selfish and the tyranny of evil men. Blessed is he who in the name of charity and goodwill shepherds the weak through the valley of darkness, for he is truly his brother's keeper and the finder of lost children. And I will strike down upon thee with great vengeance and furious anger those who attempt to poison and destroy my brothers. And you will know my name is the Lord when I lay my vengeance upon thee."

"Do you understand what we are saying to you, if you don't dese guys will cut you up and feed you to the raas rats in 'ere. We want to get our community back, we want the streets to be safe again, I'm sick and tired of hearing yet another mother crying because someone has taken her son's life, or raped her daughter. It's wankers like you that are causing this and I will fucking kill you if you carry on the way you are. You want respect, then you earn it. You want to stay around here then you behave yourself or we'll come back for you and this time we'll finish you off, because we are now looking after this community and we ain't standing for your shit no more!!!"

I wanted to kill him, there and then snuff out his useless life, but I held back, I knew we were doing this for the good of the community if I killed him then I would be no better than him, I wanted to give him a choice, he now had a choice. He could choose to carry on then we will come back or he could behave himself. I felt omnipotent, this guy's life in my hands I could squash him or let him walk, the power felt wonderful, the power of life or death.

"We'll be watching you fuck up and we is coming back for you. I don't like you, I don't like what you stand for, you're the shit I step in everyday, useless, fouling up the streets and causing a stink up my nose. Bwoy if you fuck wid us, I kill you now!" Jerry was getting really fired up, waving now the pipe wrench almost hitting both Terry and I as well. He slammed it onto the table then walked back to the tool table as if he wasn't happy with his first three selected tools.

"You don' want none of dis, you see him he wants to tek you down now, is only cos we is here dat he is calm. Is de message getting home yet, we don't want your kind on our streets fucking up our community, you want to be part of our community you straighten up or fuck off out or we'll do it for you!" Terry slapped him again.

We could hear Jerry swearing in the background and more clanking of metal on wood as he continued inspecting the array of implements on the tool table. By now Johnson's face was crimson red with blood spots around his mouth, eyes and on cuts and abrasions on his cheek from the incessant slapping. He continued to sweat profusely, he started mumbling. We couldn't hear what he was saying and had to lean down to make out his words spoken through swollen lips, he spat blood as he spoke, you could see he was in pain; every word was a struggle for him.

"Enough, enough, please don't hit me anymore. I can't take anymore. Who the fuck are you guys. I understand, I'll behave, please no more. You're going to kill me, fuck I need my stuff, I can't do this, stop. You won't hear nothing from me, please I want to go home!"

Terry turned to me, "You tink he get de message or should we beat him some more just to make sure?"

"Let me lick him wid dis if he don't get it yet he will when he taste this!" Jerry was approaching us with his newly selected tool a claw hammer. He walked into Johnson's eye line and waved it under his nose to show him what his future held for him.

"No please, please no I get it, I understand, please don't hit me, fucking hell please!" Johnson's eyes were so wide they looked like they would pop out of their sockets, they followed the claw hammer as Jerry waved it in front of him, not leaving it in case they took him by surprise and embedded themselves into his skull. I looked at Jerry, then at Terry.

"I think he understands us, I think we've made the right impression on him." Then turning to Johnson I said to him to be careful as we would be watching him, that we knew all about him, where he goes, where he slept, where he got his hits, we even knew what he ate and his inside leg measurements. I told him he couldn't mess with us and if he did he'd be back here and this time we would just leave him to, and I pointed at Jerry. He shook his head maniacally still following the claw hammer as Jerry waved it around, smiling evilly at him. He nodded his head in agreement to what I said, mumbling about how he would be good and to keep that madman away from him. He seemed contrite, he seemed like he had got the message, time would tell.

With it over I threw the sack back over his head, but this time I did not tie him up. Terry untied his hands. Meanwhile Jerry went back to the tool table to replace the tools he had taken. I saw him from the corner of my eye as I helped Johnson to his feet take a longing glance at the tools and then gently caress the claw hammer. He came back over and helped me steer Johnson out of the doorway and into the back of the van. Terry turned out the lights and locked the door, he then made furtive glances up and down the estate, still deserted, not a thing moved. He closed the back doors and jumped into the driver's seat, engine on music began to blare again playing another old school standard, we certainly had the funk.

Terry took the long way home and drove around a bit more just in case Johnson had ideas about finding the Torture Chamber later on. In the back nothing was said, we could hear Johnson breathing heavily. Jerry seemed lost in some other world so I decided not to bother him, I was glad because I was still high still on that plateau not wanting to come down, I felt that if I spoke my high would dissipate faster, so I remained quiet drinking in as much of the heady atmosphere as possible. We pulled up back by Piss-head alley. Jerry and I made sure we had our disguises on; I pulled the sack from Johnson's head while Jerry pushed the doors of the van open. No one spoke we simply looked at him and gestured that he was free to go. He quickly jumped out of the van, then stood still and looked back at us, we looked at him, Jerry was smiling, and I just glared at him. He took a deep breathe as if tasting the fresh air and the aroma coming from the alley, it tasted good to him, he nodded at us bowed his head and then he was gone, "run away little boy" was playing on the radio.

THE AFTERMATH chapter 9

Sleep was out of the question we were all still on a high. Jerry and I remained in the back of the van whilst Terry drove off, twenty minutes later he had pulled up at a bar somewhere in Ilford. We alighted from the van and went into the bar; it was empty apart from a couple sitting at the far end of the room to our left. Terry sat at a table to the right of the bar and told Jerry to get the drinks. Whilst Jerry was at the bar Terry turned to me and nodded in Jerry's direction.

"What the raas was wrong with him, I never realised that he could turn so feral, that was not the Jerry I knew, I thought at one point he was going to knock that guy's head clean off, next time we'll need to keep him on a tighter rein."

I agreed with him Jerry had scared me as well, but it was still exciting and the hairs on the back of my neck were still bristling. Terry agreed that he had been excited by the events and, if this worked with Johnson he couldn't see why we would not want to continue doing this and that we should start identifying our next target. Jerry came back with the drinks, he had a wide grin on his face, very unlike Jerry, he didn't say more than "great!" and sat down in the corner as he usually does.

We all started to laugh; soon we were in convulsive fits on the floor as we went over the events of the night. I was pretty sure we were all laughing at different parts but it was very funny and very powerful. I could not get the look on his face out of my head it reminded me of those old 1920's and 1930's films where they had black people with big grins on their faces, fat overly large lips and bulging eyes, no matter what was done to them their expressions remained the same. I remembered thinking that if I slapped him across the back of his head one more time his eyes would surely pop out.

"Listen man, that was unbelievable I did not know I could do that, the brother was scared, I'm sure he pooped himself. Man that Torture chamber is something else isn't it?" Jerry sat up and shook his head as if trying to comprehend the enormity of what just happened.

"Man I didn't recognise you back den, you was different, you weren't the Jerry I know, where did dat come from?"

"Listen man, I was just play acting, it scared him didn't it, it got the message home didn't it? Okay so I loved those tools a little bit too much, but hey!"

"Shit it scared me as well, especially when you were waving them tools around, I thought any minute now you're gonna slip and bash me or Barry."

We carried on laughing and joking for at least another thirty minutes, pulling each other's legs about things we said or did, or about the reaction of Johnson. It was a good feeling we hadn't laughed and joked like that for a long time. We had each been able to forget about our usual, mundane stuff and be a part of something we thought was great and for the common good. It was something that I had to remind Terry and Jerry about, I asked them to remember what all this was about, that it wasn't about us and the more inconspicuous we were the better.

This was for the community, for those mothers, parents who might lose someone near and dear if we were not doing this. It was for those young girls assaulted by some freak because he could do it and couldn't get her by being polite and respectful. We are doing this for the community and if what we are doing is just to gratify ourselves then we haven't changed a damn thing. I reminded them that we could not say that we had succeeded yet until we saw how Johnson Cole reacts over the next few days and possibly weeks that we had to monitor him to see how he was, then, and only then, could we slap each other on the back.

They both nodded at me, but they had that "cool it dude!" look in their eyes. They wanted to celebrate and no pontificating by me was going to spoil that moment for them. To tell the truth I wanted to as well, I soon forgot what it was all about and got loud and partied. We drank copious amounts of Rum and Brandy, plus a few slammers, we laughed a lot going over the events of the night and what more we could do, everything was great. There wasn't any point in going over what we needed to do over the next few days, like watching out for Johnson Cole or looking for our next target. Let us just enjoy the moment.

Time flew so quickly, before we knew it the bartender was chucking us out. Jerry didn't come with us, apparently he had some booty call he needed to make around the corner, he had already called her and she was waiting for him. We said our goodbyes to him and watched as he sort of floated off into the distance. Terry and I got back into the van and headed home. The radio came on and was still blaring out rare groove classics. Terry dropped me home, I gave him a hug and a big slap on the back. He drove off with another great tune ringing in my ears'

"We're gonna stand those problems all in a row and watch them fall like dominos…"

When I got in Nicolette was still up, I was a little surprised to see that she had waited up for me as I had told her that we would be late as it was a boys' night out. I hadn't told her what we were really getting up to, I'm not actually sure that she would've approved and would more than likely try and talk me out of it, plus I didn't want her to worry. I could imagine the amount of missed calls on my phone because she would be fretting, I didn't want that. She seemed happy enough and had a cup of hot chocolate ready for me. We spent the next ten minutes in small talk, the usual stuff, how was your day, put away any bad guys, how's the corporate world, kids got off alright, how was the boys' night out, did you guys sort out Jerry's problems? All the while all I kept thinking about was whether all that macho stuff with Johnson Cole was better than sex.

Before I knew it I had the largest erection I had ever had, Nicolette must have noticed the stirring in my loins because before I knew it she was on top of me night dress going north and we were making love on the kitchen table, mad, noisy love. So loud it woke the kids, we got them back to bed and to sleep and resumed were we had left off, Nicolette on top of me. This time she had discarded her nightdress and her lithe brown skin was all over me. I lay back, closed my eyes and caressed every inch of her skin, she orgasmed there and then, long and loud, but we hadn't finished it was my turn on top, then from behind then over the bed head, we took positions directly from the Kama Sutra. When I finally climaxed I realised I had lied; what had happened with Johnson Cole wasn't better than sex. We fell asleep in each others arms naked and sweaty and happy, ecstatically so.

Terry told me during one of our one on ones that he had experienced more or less the same thing. It had been in his mind that nothing, not even sex could replace the feeling of power, electricity running through his body, but that night with Eva was probably on par with anything they had ever experienced. He told me that it was the whole cocktail of emotions mixed up that went off with a bang that night. He had tried to repeat the feeling since but it hasn't been the same. He understood we needed to wait and was patient whilst we kept watch on Johnson and looked for our next target.

Over the next few days I spotted Johnson Cole at Court on two occasions, he was no longer the brash loud mouth, he seemed timid, eager to please, sat down in a corner and remained quiet whilst waiting for his sentence. In court he was politeness itself. You could see that he was still using, but Rome wasn't built in a day they say, but he had certainly changed. I managed to keep an eye on him for about two evenings, even though he visited his usual haunts he wasn't picking fights or shoving people or being loud and disrespectful, this guy had really changed, our plan seems to have worked. I made sure that I kept Terry and Jerry updated and told them how he now was. I had even overheard a remark from one of the regulars at the Shooting Star who was asking his friend what had happened to Cole.

"Wha'ppen to him man, is like a whole new man, him jus' ask me to excuse him, normally him a jus' push and shove. Smaddy mussa gi' him a good slap for him to behave like dis now don't you t'ink?"

Johnson Cole was our first success and there were a few more, we were on a roll. It wasn't until we had seen how he would behave, not just for a day or two but for a week, two weeks before we started to look for the next target. It was only Jerry who kept pushing for more action. The problem he had is that he did not come into contact with anyone likely to be a target. He had asked his son Nelson a few pointed questions but he just got suspicious and clammed up, only saying that the only bad boy he knew had already got his comeuppance, that he did not move in those circles, and why was he all of a sudden so interested. So Jerry had to rely on Terry and I and he had to wait to sample those tools again. We both reminded him that we were not doing this for our own gratification that this was a mission and it should not be rushed.

Jerry was behaving like an addict who had his first taste of a new designer drug, he wanted more and he wanted it now, he couldn't wait. Unfortunately for him he couldn't do it alone he needed Terry and I, he even needed Alton Weekes. We didn't need his constant cajoling everyday, but we managed to keep him focussed on the aim. For him this meant bedding even more women, if he wasn't out drinking with us he was with yet another booty call. It seemed the longer he had to wait the more he used sex to re-create the feeling he had that night both during the chastising of Johnson Cole and after when he went on his booty call. But, the more he had sex the more he wanted to be back in the torture chamber. At least it kept him off our backs for a while.

AARON TRENDWAY chapter 10

It was three weeks after Johnson Cole that I met up with Terry who gave me a name to look up on the company computer and to find out anything I could about him. He would not tell me what he had done; simply that he fits the bill for what we were looking for. I checked his name on the PNC there was a hit. I was a little puzzled as he only had three previous convictions, one for assault, one for possession of a bladed article and one minor driving offence. He certainly did not seem at first glance that there was anything about him. I gave Terry the news, he didn't seem put off by it and he continued to refuse to tell me anything until we met up the next night, I was intrigued.

I did some digging around of my own, speaking with the prosecutor who had last dealt with Trendway to try and get some insight into him. She could barely remember him, all that she could recall was that he was medium height five foot eight, medium build, reasonably handsome (if you like that sort of thing!), and reasonably polite, totally unremarkable. She asked me why, I told her simply a friend's son had some issue with him and I was just checking him out. She replied that was unusual as if it is the guy she remembered he was a bit of a coward more into ladies, would say silly things like 'I'm a lover not a fighter' thought of himself a bit of a Michael Jackson, so him having beef with another guy was unusual. I was more intrigued.

We met at the usual place at the usual time, I got there first and bought a drink for Terry and myself, sat down with newspaper and waited for Terry to show. I knew Jerry was not coming he had already cried off as he had some booty call or something to attend to, which seemed to suit Terry as he wanted to discuss Aaron Trendway with me and I was keen to find out why he thought he was a suitable target.

I had become engrossed in my newspaper; reading some article about a community leader who had made great strides in rehabilitating young black boys who had been expelled and kicked out of mainstream education. He had taught them respect and the importance of learning and they had come around to his methods and were now behaving themselves and doing well academically, or at least better than they could every imagine they would do. The story had enthralled me because in a round about way this was exactly what we were doing, turning round the mindset of the worst in our community, teaching them respect for their family and community and helping them to realise that this was better for them and the community that they behave themselves and make themselves one with the community. Just that this guy preaches hard love, abstinence, religion and hard work, we preach the same just that it entails them feeling the true force of the community, just in case they needed that little push.

The difference was he could laud it with newspapers and politicians and explain, in detail what it was he was doing and produce his mission statement for all to see. We could not do this, because we knew that what we were doing was illegal because we used force to compel change. I rationalised in my mind that the government, the police etc, did use force to compel citizens to obey the law in various ways. And if you didn't conform you would feel the full force of the law both metaphorically and painfully; just like the poll tax rioters, the Brixton rioters, right back to the Tolpuddle Martyrs, even the ANC and Nelson Mandela. I knew in my own mind that we had the high ground, but we walked a tightrope and some would call us vigilantes, but I was convinced that we were not vigilantes. This wasn't some hastily assembled posse out to avenge some crime or other, who on locating the hunted would take the law into their own hands and kill in the name of the law.

Things had got so bad with the lawlessness in the community that I doubted if anyone would accuse us of that type of behaviour. I had convinced myself, especially with the ongoing change in Johnson Cole that we would be lauded and praised for our work in the community. Just as with the guy I was reading about, mothers, schools the whole establishment would supply us with names in order to regulate them, we are doing a community service and legality should not get in the way of that.

Terry woke me from my thoughts by slamming his bag down hard on the table. He sat down hard and sighed a huge sigh, picked up the drink I had bought for him and downed it in one. He sat still for a while looking into the bottom of his glass, before I could ask him what was wrong he asked if I wanted another, got up from his seat and went to the bar. I watched him slope off, he looked liked he had the troubles of the world on his shoulders, gone was the chest out preening cock of the last few weeks, I wondered if he was having family problems. He came back with the drinks and again slouched back in his chair and sighed heavily again. Knowing Terry I knew if I pressed him he would clam up and find an excuse to leave, so I waited for him to compose himself and tell me in his own time. He knocked back the next drink just as quickly, I went to the bar for a refill for him as I hadn't even touched the drink he had bought for me.

"She ain't a bad girl, just didn't make the right choices early in life. Had shites for parents who didn't give a damn more interested in where the next drink was coming from than looking after their children. Her mother just popped them out and left them to social services to look after. She's got six brothers and sisters; she was the first, all the others somewhere in care. She came to me because she didn't want to be like her mother wanted to live life and also wanted to trace her brothers and sisters. She'd made mistakes got pregnant at fifteen, her kid's three now, but she wanted to get her life back on track."

"Who are you talking about?"

"Sorry mate, a girl who has been helping out at the centre, she came about a year ago, an absolute godsend, knows the language of the kids has experienced so much in her short life, made mistakes and has now started to give back to the community, her name is Tamina Webster, I'm sure you've met her when you've been to the centre?"

"Short mixed raced girl, thin legs, good tits, yeah I remember her, got a bit of a gob on her, but seems to mean well, she was in the other day shouting at a group of girls, is that the one?"

"Yep that's her, she was shouting at them because she had caught them smoking herbs in the toilets. Been having baby father problems, but I didn't realise how bad things were until the other day. His name is Aaron Trendway and I think he should be our next target, the bastard needs regulating!"

I was surprised by this, if we went around targeting people just because they were not nice and polite to their girlfriends, just because we know their girlfriends, we would be just as bad as them. I tried to tell Terry this and remind him what this was all about; it certainly wasn't for personal vendettas. I told him that I had checked this guy out, but apart from some minor crap he had nothing on him and certainly didn't seem like the sort of person that we would be interested in. I told him that if he wanted me to take this seriously he needed to elaborate and give me a better reason than what he had given so far. I told him the fact was that we were not here to solve relationship problems.

He told me that it was probably easier for her to tell me directly but that he didn't want to put her through it again. She hadn't been herself for a while and he had kept asking her what the problem was, she would just tell him that 'Trendy' that was his street name, was being a prat and hassling her. He wasn't interested in the child he wanted to get back with her. Terry told me how they had split up acrimoniously because he didn't want to work but wanted to live up to his street name and always have the best clothes, etc and then there was the womanising. Apparently she had found out that he had two other baby mothers, plus a string of other conquests. I told Terry that he sounded like a Jerry clone. Terry admonished me telling me that this wasn't the time for humour.

"Only he wasn't just hassling the girl. He had basically held her captive for three days over last weekend, put a gun to her head. She had let him in because he said he wanted to see his kid and wanted his mum to spend some time with the boy. She let him take him for a couple of hours; he came back without him, that's when he put the gun to her head. Said the boy was with his mother who was having him for the weekend. He told her that she was going to look after him for the weekend that if she didn't she would never see her kid again. He beat her up making sure he didn't mark her face and repeatedly raped her for the whole weekend. She had to cook for him and do whatever he told her. Before he fell asleep he would tie her up, in the morning he would untie her and demand his breakfast then repeat the whole thing again."

I could understand Terry's anger and pain, but I told him that this still smelt of revenge rather than a community thing and though I shared his outrage I did not think that this was something the Star Chamber could get involved in, it was too personal. He just looked at me and carried on. He told me that he knew my search wouldn't come up with anything, because he had done some snooping as well. The guy thought he was a player, but he didn't know the meaning of being a player, he certainly wasn't Jerry.

"Look man I understand what you mean about it being personal, but you have to listen. I believe this guy is our next target, because it is not only Tamina he's done this to, he's a serial rapist, girls are afraid of him. He's a confidence trickster, he looks good smells good, talks the talk and, unfortunately, girls fall for it, but he doesn't like straight sex, he's a sadist. Once he's lured them in then he works on their mind and he's believable. Tamina told me about a few other girls who had opened up to her because she knew him, all too afraid to go to the police. Apparently, there is a story about one girl who disappeared from the area. She was targeted by him, fell for him and he did his sadistic routine on her, but she fought back and threatened to go to the police, he didn't touch her but her mother, who was a nurse and worked shifts was hospitalised a couple of days later, she was beaten to a pulp as she walked home from work. Of course her bag was stolen so police thought it was a robbery, a mugging gone bad because she fought back. The very next day 'Trendy' had approached the girl, roughed her up and showed her a brooch which she knew was her mother's and had been taken off her during the 'robbery'. Of course, she never went to the police, but her and her family quickly moved out of the area."

With all that I had come around, this guy sounded very much like our next target. However, I needed to know for certain that it was not just a story; I didn't want to regulate someone on tall tales from the Street. Terry saw it coming.

"Tamina knows the girl and was still in contact with her, her family had moved to Croydon, I spoke with her on the phone two days ago. She was very reticent to talk to me at first, but Tamina told her it was okay and nothing would get back to him. I had to explain to Tamina that I might know of people who could keep him away from her, but that I needed more to go on, that it wasn't just her because it would get back to them. I told her that I needed to know that he did this for kicks, that there were more victims so that he couldn't trace it back to her and then to them. This is why she gave me this girl and I was able to talk to her. She told me the story about her Mother and how she still gets headaches a year later and was still off work. She hated him, but I could still tell that she was frightened. That's why I think he's our target and I'm sure that Jerry would agree, what do you say?"

I couldn't do anything else but agree, I told Terry that as he seemed to have made some enquiries about him that he should set up the appropriate place and time for this. He told me that it had to be very soon, in the next few days because heaven knows who else he was going to terrorise or he may go back to Tamina. He told me that he had been escorting her home since she told him what had happened and that she triple locks her doors in case he came around. He hadn't been around for a few days maybe he's got another girl locked up. I agreed, but told him that we needed to know his hang outs and where best to get at him. I would meet up with Jerry the next day and inform him to be ready for action.

Terry went to the bar to buy another round of drinks, I thought about our next victim Aaron 'Trendy' Trendway. I thought about the community leader and how he would deal with him, would 'hard love' work, would cajoling him about respect have any effect on him, would teaching him community values mean he would not force himself on another woman, whose way would be more effective up against an animal like this?

Of course, when I told Jerry he was excited. I described what Terry had told me about him and about my initial reticence that we should not do it if it was personal and what we were all about. Jerry didn't agree his take on it was that even if he had only attacked Tamina that was cause enough for us to act.

"Listen man, it's shits like him we need to regulate, he's liable to do more harm to someone before the police could act, if we don't do anything and he does hurt or kill someone how are you going to feel, the longer bastards like him stay untouched the more people they are gonna hurt, I'm with Terry let's get him and get him soon!"

Two days later I got a call from Terry, he and Jerry were in the van and were ready to regulate Trendy. He confirmed that he knew where he was and it should be quite easy to pick him up. He picked me up at the top of my road and explained the plan to me. He lived on Pretoria Road, which was a quiet road near the School. He never normally left his flat until after eight o'clock, so we had the cover of darkness. We needed to get to Pretoria Road by eight o'clock and wait for him to leave his house. When he left he would normally jump in his car and head off towards the High Road, we had to get him between leaving his house and getting into his car. He normally parked his car nearer to the corner so he had a little walk before he got to it. Jerry and I were to jump him the same as with Johnson Cole, as soon as we had him Terry would pull the van up in order that we could bundle him in as quickly as possible.

They picked me up at seven thirty, I heard them from around the corner as Terry blasted out an old jazz funk standard. I could see him and Jerry nodding their heads in time to the music. We had time to go over the plan, to make sure nothing went wrong, Terry drove to Pretoria Road to ensure we got the right parking place, we saw his car parked about twenty metres from his flat and just in front of it was a space big enough to park the van, everything was ideal. We sat in the van trying to look inconspicuous to the odd person walking by walking their dog, or coming home from work, or going to the pub, no-one seemed to notice us. We heard a door slam, Terry looked into the wing mirror, it was him right on cue. He stopped at his doorway, he was engrossed in a phone call, his mobile phone seemed fixed to his ear, he didn't notice Jerry and I climb out of the front of the van and open the back doors. He walked slowly to his car still engrossed in his phone call oblivious to all going on around him. The problem was we couldn't grab him until he finished his call, and hopefully he would do that before he drove off.

"Hey babes you know I love you, yeah sweetness, course, I'll be round soon just hold on a little while more for the Trendster. Yeah, I know you love your Trendy, you want it, you want me. I can't wait, I'll be there soon. Listen if you don't hang up Trendy's gonna take longer to come. Yeah I know you like it that way, yeah, yeah okay see yah soon…"

As soon as he hung up he took his car keys from his pocket. He had a wry smile on his face, a self satisfied smug look, the look of someone who knew he was onto a promise that night. Before he could put his hands on the door handle Jerry and I had swooped. As with Johnson Cole Jerry threw the sack over his head and I quickly wrapped tape around the sack and his torso, at the same time Jerry was punching and kicking him. I lifted him off his feet and threw him into the van; I was surprised how light he was. We slammed the doors shut and banged on the side of the van to alert Terry who took off towards the Torture Chamber. It went smoothly, we were certainly faster than the last time, Trendy didn't have time to breathe let alone shout out. It took him five minutes before he spoke a muffled sound coming from inside the sack.

"What you wants with me, I ain't done nothing to yous, who are yous? Do you know who I am?"

Jerry kicked and punched him hard and asked him who he was, and told him he'd find out soon what we want with him, that he likes inflicting pain so he'll love what we had planned for him.

It wasn't long before we had arrived at the Torture Chamber, Jerry and I waited for Terry to open the doors then we bundled Trendy out of the van and escorted him to the small chair and table in the middle of the chamber. I tied his hands to the chair and removed the sack from over his head. He was sweating profusely and blinking madly at the light above his head. His eyes darted around the chamber then at Terry, then to me and back again. He started swearing and shouting for help and struggled, thrashing around in the chair trying to get free. From the corner of my eye I saw Jerry approach us with something in his hand, something big and metallic, he swung it and caught Trendy on the side of his head just above his ear. There was a loud thud the sound of metal on bone, metal won and Trendy was quiet, but he continued to struggle. Blood began to pour from the wound just above his ear, his eyes bulged as he felt the warm blood seeping over his ear and down his neck, we had his attention.

Terry was the first to speak, he tried to contain his anger so spoke through gritted teeth, his voice was dark and evil.

"So, you fucking like beating and forcing yourself on girls den huh, you fucking lickle snake. When we done wid you you gonna wish you ain't reach puberty yet. You is dog shit and me is gonna walk all over you and squash you into de ground!"

"Why you doing this to me I ain't done nutting to yous, let me loose you fucking bastards!"

Jerry had returned and dropped a variety of tools onto the small table, he and Terry began selecting the tools of their choice. Terry leaned over and whispered into his ear.

"I'm going to use this" and he raised a large steel body clamp which he waved in front of him. "This I'm gonna use on your bollocks I'm gonna tighten it until your bollocks pop!"

"Or maybe we just cut them off and shove them in your mouth, how you like that" Jerry interjected waving a large knife in front of him.

"Fuck off you bastards let me go, noooo, leave me alone!" Trendy was in tears, but was still struggling.

He struggled even more as Jerry leaned over him and pulled down his trousers and smashed the body clamp down onto the edge of the chair narrowly missing his privates. The force of the body clamp on the chair knocking off a chunk of wood sending the splinter flying up and catching Trendy on the chin. Now he was still daring not to move in case the next blow really did smash into his penis and testicles. He seemed to be praying, hoping for some sort of divine intervention. Jerry looked at him through the braids on his hat and asked him.

"Am I my brother's keeper?"

Terry then repeated the question to him; he looked puzzled and afraid all at the same time. Terry had picked up a large sledgehammer and rammed it into Trendy's stomach, the force made him retch and throw up his last meal. It spewed out from his mouth into his lap and down his bare legs.

"I'm gonna make you lick that all up!" and Jerry tried to force his head down into his lap, but he wasn't that supple.

Terry leaned over again and as Jerry was forcing down his head gave him an uppercut connecting just under his chin and forcing his head back, the force of which almost broke the back of the chair. I stood back even further watching Terry and Jerry work him over. I tried to speak but couldn't the sheer violence, the whole situation had rendered me speechless. They were really doing a number on him and all he could do was simply soak up the punishment. I wasn't very happy with what was going on, but I couldn't stop them. Something flashed through my mind and then remained, I couldn't shake it. They wanted to kill him, but killing was not what we were about, we are supposed to just regulate them. If we killed him we were no better than them, we become vigilantes and we will be hunted by the police. I could see the headlines in the newspapers now.

"VIGILANTE KILLERS ON THE LOOSE"

I had to stop them before they killed him, but there was no way that I could use force. I went right up behind Trendy and held my arms out and shouted as loud as I could for them to stop, wait, listen to me before this got out of hand.

"I think he's had enough now we have to talk to him, let him know why he is here, we don't want to kill the bastard do we?"

Terry and Jerry stopped in mid swing, there eyes were wild, I could see that they didn't want to stop but my imploring struck a chord and they came down momentarily. Jerry was the first to speak; he agreed with me and motioned to Terry to hold off a minute. He still had the body clamp in his hand; he put it under Trendy's chin and forced his head up. Terry slammed the sledgehammer down on the table, they got his attention. I held his head up and turned it so he could see me by his side. I spoke to him in measured terms.

"Do you want to die tonight? If you don't then you have to listen to me. We know what you do, we know you are scum, we know you like to force yourself on women; we know you like to lock them up and use them. This stops now or we kill you now or another day, it's your choice. The community do not want you, you gotta shape up or you are dead, do you understand me?"

Terry interjected, "It is my fucking wish that you die, and I want to be the one to rid the streets of you, make it a lickle safer for my daughter dem, you is a dead man walking. We is watching your raas, day and night, you nasty fucking dawg!"

Jerry just stood looking at him still with the body clamp under his chin.

He was sweating profusely and his braided wig was hanging half off his head. Terry motioned for him to put the clamp down. Before he put it down he slammed it into Trendy's exposed pubic region. Trendy's eyes bulged, his mouth opened wide as if to scream but no sound came out. His head then dropped and he let out an inaudible sigh and passed out.

Jerry then spoke, "Listen, this t'ing don't deserve to live there ain't nothing we can do to him to mek him stop cos it's in him, hurting women is a part of him, he couldn't live without doing it. I tink we should extinguish him and we can do the world a favour"

Terry agreed with him and said one swing of this hammer in the right place and we will put him out of his misery. I argued long and hard that it was not a decision that is ours to make, we do not have divine right to do this. That it was not what we had signed up to do. I repeated my fears to them, that we would become a posse and that we would be just as bad as those hooded freaks hunting a man down and stringing him up onto a tree, just because there was something that we did not like about them. I argued that we had done what we set out to do, we had given him a feel of his own medicine and told him why we were doing it and what we wanted of him, this was all we could do. After this all we could hope for is that he either regulates himself, or someone gives evidence against him and he is locked up. The chances of the latter were slim he had something on these women who were scared to speak to the police about him. Our job now is to watch him and see whether he regulates himself, if not he is back here, we cannot be his judge and executioner that is not what this is about.

I think they both agreed, but I could see in their eyes that they wanted to continue to hurt this guy. I could understand what they were feeling and I almost agreed with Jerry, but we had signed up to something else not murder. I untied his hands and he slumped to the floor his face was a bloody mess. I pulled up his trousers and then tied the sack around his head. Terry went outside to warm up the van, I heard the engine start up and simultaneously music began blaring from the speakers.

"Can you handle it, can you handle it..."

Jerry had begun returning the tools to the table in the corner. I stood over Trendy waiting for Jerry to finish, I almost felt sorry for him, but he was lucky if I had not intervened he would probably be dead now, he should be grateful. Jerry came back and we lifted him up and threw him into the back of the van.

"...Cos you ain't had nothing like it..."

I did not feel the same exhilaration as I did with Johnson Cole, I was high and the atmosphere was definitely heady, but it wasn't the same for me. Jerry was happy and was singing along to the radio and banging on the wall of the van in rhythm to the music. Terry was also singing they both seemed happy with their work.

We dropped Trendy, literally back to his flat. Terry pulled up outside his flat, turned the music down, in case it disturbed a neighbour, we waited a few minutes to ensure no one was around, then simply untied him, took the sack off his head and bundled him out off the van, he was still unconscious. Jerry shut the back doors and went round to sit in the front of the van leaving me in the back. I could hear the two of them laughing and joking, they were certainly happy. I had some thinking to do. We pulled up at the same pub and went in for a drink. Jerry got the drinks in, he and Terry stood at the bar still high from earlier, laughing and joking about Trendy.

I wasn't so enthralled, I admitted to myself that I was scared that it had got out of hand; I didn't want to be a murderer but, at the same time I had come to the conclusion that maybe they were right, maybe the best thing for all was to have got rid of Trendy once and for all. I was coming around to the conclusion that he would not stop, because that type of behaviour was him and no beating was going to make him regulate his behaviour.

Terry and Jerry sat down, they noticed that I was quiet and pensive and urged me to speak to them, tell them what was on my mind. I explained my dilemma, that I thought they had gone too far, but equally I understood the predicament, that this guy, no matter what we did to him, was going to attack someone else. That sort of deviant behaviour was very much part of him, it is his DNA. But, I explained we are not killers and never set out on this road to become vigilantes. We were doing this to protect the community, make those attacking the community think again about their actions because, we representing the community, were fighting back, fighting fire with fire. The problem that we now face is how do we know that this guy is not doing these things to women, if he is scaring them that much that they are not talking how are we going to know.

"It is just messy, do we grab him every time we see him with a women, or what are you going to do Terry if you see him talking to Tamina, you can't assume that he's up to no good, because, remember they have history, they have a kid together, this ain't the way it's suppose to go, we should have the answers!"

They both nodded assent to what I was saying, terry added that, if it comes to it then we should pick him up every week just to remind him that we were watching him.

"And believe me, he ain't ever gonna get used to us beating the shit out of him every week. I could beat that raas hole up every fucking day, you hear me Jerry?"

"Listen, it would be my pleasure to fuck him up every week, if that is what we have to do then so be it!"

We had a few more drinks whilst we pontificated about the morality of Trendy, then headed off home. I was looking forward to making love to my wife, I didn't have the same heady feelings as before, I really just wanted her to hold me, for her to tell me that she loved me and reassure me that everything was alright in our world. Jerry, of course, went on a booty call, slapping us both on the back as a goodbye laughing out loud as he left us.

Music was blaring out in the van; I was still quiet and left Terry to sing the choruses of his favourite tunes. "Make my funk the P funk I want to funk with you..." Whilst I tried to figure out a way of monitoring Trendy's behaviour, nothing came apart from the boys' suggestion to drag him in on a weekly basis and give him a slap just for being alive. To make him thank the Lord he was alive and forget about his deviant ways. I just could not see it happening; we had to come up with something radical.

My head started to hurt, I didn't want to think about it anymore, I needed to switch off, calm down before I got home. I turned to Terry and asked him what he was doing over the next few days, he didn't answer so engrossed was he in the jazz funk classic blaring from the radio. I had to nudge him twice to get his attention, and then once I did I forgot what I wanted to ask him. He looked at me puzzled then carried on singing and playing his imaginary saxophone with one hand and holding the steering wheel with the other. I left him to it and tried to enjoy the music as well, but my head continued to ache. 'What if' kept running through my mind, not really a question, more of a rhetorical statement regarding what had just transpired and what was likely to happen, this really was a conundrum.

TAMINA WEBSTER chapter 11

Over the next few days I had quite a few conversations with Terry and Jerry about the Trendy dilemma. Jerry was quite sanguine about the whole thing, I think it was just because he fancied beating on the guy some more and the thought of doing it weekly seemed to illicit the beast from deep within him. Terry was a little more worried and confirmed to me that he had been watching Tamina more closely than before, for signs of any abuse or that Trendy had been bothering her. He confided in me that he was concerned for her because Trendy definitely had a hold on her.

Her mother was from an Indian family and father was from a Caribbean family and got together at a time when the two communities did not mix. Her mother was disowned by her family for dating and getting impregnated by a black man. They would ignore her if they passed her in the street, father, mother, sisters, brothers – the whole family. It was probably this that made her turn to drink and drugs. Her father was already selling drugs on street corners and even at the local college which is where they had met, he called out to her "hey my dusky beauty!" she responded by batting her eyelids and trying to walk seductively as she past him. Eventually, they would meet up clandestinely after college and at weekends, she would tell her parents that she was doing extra work in college or around a friends house, one acceptable to them. It was when she fell pregnant with Tamina that the whole truth came out and she was banished from the family home and everyone forbidden to talk to her or even acknowledge her existence. Things were pretty hard for her, a young baby, living in a flat on the 10th floor of a tower block, a man who was never at home preferring to spend time with friends or selling drugs. Only coming home at the crack of dawn demanding sex. It seemed to Tamina that her mother always blamed her for the life she lived, and then as she dropped more children blamed each one of them for her continuing plight, then took more drink and drugs to forget her plight and her growing number of children.

She had also explained about her connection with Trendy, he was her first real love, spoke to her and treated her the 'right way', so much so that they had a son together. He didn't ignore her he gave her attention, something she had never really had before. He was three years older than her when they met; she was fourteen and he seventeen. She had confided in Terry that sex with him was rough, but she quite liked it. He never ever meant to hurt her, but when things get so rough in the heat of passion you do get a few knocks and bruises. But he was good to her that was until the baby came along, whilst she was heavily pregnant and really not in the mood for sex he would force himself on her. Even after giving birth and being in labour for thirty six hours, a week later he wanted sex and took it, not seeming to care that she was in pain and bleeding, after throwing her a towel and order her to clean herself up. This whole thing carried on for a few months and he seemed to get bored of the mundane life of having a child around getting in the way when he wanted sex and he disappeared from her life for a good few months. He never showed any interest in the child, if he cried he would give her a wilting look as if to say, stop him now. If he was dirty or needed feeding he would simply call Tamina. She also noticed that he would never pick up or hold him, or show him any attention, fatherhood did not suit him.

He started contacting her again when the boy was two, after bumping into her at the Community centre. He had apparently gone there to meet another girl, but ignored her when he saw Tamina. They hooked up again, seems his type of rough sex was infectious. Three months later they split up again after she found out he had other baby mothers whom he was still seeing, plus other women who would constantly ring his phone even when they were together. She had told Terry that sex with him now was a lot rougher and he seemed to take much too much pleasure in just inflicting pain.

She had originally come to the centre because she found out that two of her younger siblings often frequented it. She had asked Terry to organise a meeting with them for her. They were twelve and thirteen and Terry was impressed how she handled herself with them, as they first refused to acknowledge her. They had been fostered out from very young and had not seen their mother or their other siblings for many years. It wasn't long before they were inseparable meeting up most days at the Centre.

She was there so often that Terry and the others asked her if she wanted a part time role caring for some of the other children, which she gratefully accepted. She threw herself into the work of the centre so much so that they got her onto a counselling course, which she passed with top marks. She was very much part of the team and the other children looked up to her.

This is when she began to open up to Terry telling him about her upbringing, moving from children's home to foster home and back again. How she narrowly avoided ending up a drunk like her mother and hating herself for the life she lived. She had told him that she was into self harming and how she would always have a pair of scissors with her so that when things got particular dark or bad for her she would slash her arms and body so that the dark feelings would go away, with the pain and the blood.

This self harming and the need for pain Terry hypothesised, was probably why she was drawn to Trendy, he gave her pleasure and pain all at the same time. The fact that he inflicted the pain on her meant that she was useful and someone wanted her. She had associated pain with life and the fact that someone took away the need for her to hurt herself she associated with love, the more he hurt her, the more she thought that he loved her. Being at the centre, finding some of her siblings and seeing other people in need and being able to help them gave her a different perspective on life. It showed her that she didn't need to be in pain and that love is unconditional.

Each time she tried to pull herself out, Trendy would appear back into her life and the more he did the more she realised with all her new discoveries that he just wasn't good for her. Telling Terry about the last incident was therapeutic for her and she now wanted to get him out of her life. Terry had hinted to her that something had happened to Trendy, that he had been visited, by what he called, 'concerned citizens' and hopefully he had taken on board the message he had been given. He implored her to let him know if he tried anything inappropriate. She was grateful to him for his help, she did not ask who the 'concerned citizens' were or what they did.

I had various conversations with Terry over the next week, mainly for him to give me updates on Trendy and to talk about any other possible targets. He told me that he had been asking Tamina if she had heard or seen him, but she had not, not even a text message. She told him that she had been tempted to call or text him, but Terry had warned her off this as for someone like him it might be construed as a green light for him to turn up again, it was better she left it as it was.

Terry had told me that he had driven past his flat on a couple of occasions after work and that he had seen his light on, so he was still around, but it looked like he was laying low. This news didn't fill me with satisfaction and I told Terry that if he was laying low, that he was probably licking his wounds and once he had healed he would be back on the prowl, it didn't augur well. I told him that he needed to keep a close watch on Tamina, that even if she was a few minutes late to be concerned, I didn't trust this guy one little bit. Terry told me that I was overreacting that the fact he was laying low was a good sign and not to keep worrying so much.

In the bar with Terry and Jerry a week later Terry told us that Tamina had a new boyfriend and she seemed the happiest she had been for ages. She had met him on the counselling course, but had blocked all his attempts to take her out, but she told Terry that as Trendy was 'out of the way' she felt more confident and finally acceded to go out with this guy. He was about five years older but seemed to have his head screwed on and seemed normal, especially compared to Trendy.

"Michael Jackson is normal when put next to that guy!" Jerry had retorted.

We were all glad for her it was about time that she had some good news. Terry confirmed that there was still nothing from Trendy. It was then that Jerry told us that he had seen Trendy in the West End just two days ago going into some clothes shop on Oxford Street. His head was still bandaged, but other than that he seemed fine. Both Terry and I yelled at him, did he not think that we would want to know this little snippet of information a bit earlier. He simply shrugged his shoulders saying that he didn't think we were that concerned. Besides the little shit was on his own, probably replacing the trousers we ruined with his blood, piss and shit. And anyway, if he hasn't tried to contact Tamina in all this time it means he's taken us seriously.

We had to agree with him, it certainly seemed promising. Terry was all for us targeting him again in the next few days, just to make sure that he understood where we were coming from. Jerry agreed and suggested that we do it on Wednesday. I was not too sure it was my view that if he seemed to be behaving himself and he certainly hadn't contacted Tamina we should let it lie and just keep an eye on him. In the end they persuaded me that we should 'remind him' and we should do it on Wednesday. I asked them to ensure one thing, which was to lessen the violence on him, he was already scared all we needed was to threaten the same violence or worse than before to reinforce the message, they both agreed.

I also advised them that I was looking at three possible targets for the future, but nothing was concrete yet. All three had court cases in the next few days and they could all go down. However, I told them that it was unlikely because there had been mistakes made with the arrests and subsequent mistakes by my peers in the Crown Prosecution Service. Certainly two of them will be ideal targets, but I did not want to tell them any more yet in case things changed. They both seemed happy with this and Jerry made a toast to our future targets.

"May they see the light of their errant ways, or feel the force of Jerry and his tools!"

We all laughed at this, I'm sure that Terry had the same image in his mind of Jerry calmly trying out various tools on the tool table, then smiling contentedly once he found the right one. Terry asked Jerry what his fascination was with the tool table. Jerry simply said;

"Phallic symbols man, swinging them things around give me power, gets my testosterone racing and gives me a boner, don't you guys get the same feeling, I'm sure you do?!"

I did not want to admit to having the same feelings, so I laughed with him but did not say anything. Terry looked a bit embarrassed but agreed with Jerry that it had the same affect on him. I attempted to explain the psychology of power and used dictators like Idi Amin to prove my point. They had all taken power and probably started off with some altruistic notion of helping their nation and people, then they notice the power they had, people were actually scared of them. They would think, 'blimey I was a wimp at school, I was never good with women, people in my neighbourhood used to laugh at me." Then all of a sudden they had this power, they dictated whether someone lived or died, they could have all the finest things in life. Very soon altruism all but dies and it becomes about them. Of course, they had their minions who fed them lines about how great they were. The more sycophantic they were the more they got from their divine leader and the more they sucked up. Power does that to you and the power of what we are doing will have that effect on you.

They both looked at me with puzzled expression and asked me what I was talking about. "What the fuck was all that about man, you know you think too much you need to get a life and do something more worthwhile." was Terry's response. Jerry simply looked at me and shook his head, then raised his empty glass and waved me away to the bar. Whilst at the Bar Terry got a phone call, I looked over because he normally turns his phone off when we were drinking, so I was a little surprised. He did not say much but he looked concerned.

"Okay, okay, wait there I'm coming right now. No don't do nothing I'll be there in five minutes!"

"Hey what's up what's the problem?"

"That was Tamina, she is in trouble something to do with that bastard Trendy, got to go to hers now!"

"What the fuck?"

Jerry and I told him that we were coming to, it sounded like he needed back up. We jumped into Terry's car and headed off with a screech of his tyres. He didn't say a word through the whole journey. We got to Tamina's in three minutes. We turned right from Grove Green Road into Drayton Road then a right again then first left into Chelmsford Road, towards the bottom of the road we pulled up outside a four storey block of flats. Terry jumped out of the car and ran towards the main entrance, we could see Tamina standing at the door, she was wearing a purple knee length dressing gown, which had embroidered dark purple and red flowers on each side, the dressing gown was tied tightly by a purple coloured belt the gown and the tight belt seemed to be fighting to restrain her large breast which looked like they could fall out at any time, it looked like that was all she was wearing. Jerry and I joined them and stood a few feet away. She was sobbing uncontrollably, we could see bruising on her wrists and she had the start of a black eye, which carried on swelling up right before or eyes. Terry pulled her to him and tried to console her. She managed to control her sobbing to some extent and pointed to an open door to a flat on the ground floor. Terry was asking her where Trendy was, she pointed again to the flat and said he's in there sobbing as she said this.

Terry was the first to enter followed quickly by Jerry and I Tamina remained outside. We were expecting to see Trendy facing us off holding some sort of weapon, a knife, a chair leg, something, but there was three of us and we would simply rush him, disarm him, beat him up then drag him out from Tamina's home. However, we were not confronted by Trendy, instead the Lounge looked like a bomb had gone off inside it. Furniture was either turned upside down or broken, curtains were ripped and hanging from their rails, this was the scene of a violent struggle. Jerry then called us; he had found a trail of blood in the hallway leading from the street door down the hallway to the kitchen. We followed the trail of blood to the kitchen. The kitchen was also completely wrecked, the floor was strewn with cutlery and broken crockery. It was a small kitchen with conventional sink and drainer worktops on the two longest sides, a stand alone Parkinson Cowan gas cooker with eye level grill. The washing machine was sited adjacent to the sink and to the right of it was the fridge freezer which just about fitted into the alcove.

The door to the washing machine was broken and water was still flooding out onto the floor and mixing with the blood to form a foaming red stream flowing away from the body of Trendy sitting up propped between the washing machine and the fridge freezer. We all, simultaneously, took a step back. I rubbed my eyes thinking this was a dream. There lay Trendy with a kitchen knife stuck deep between his ribs, all that was showing was the black coloured handle of the knife. He was dressed only his boxer shorts, white ones which had now turned red. His eyes were wide open and looked at us pleading with us to take the knife out and revive him, but we knew just by looking at him that he had already gone from this mortal world. His hands lay lifeless by his side, we could make out many slash marks on his hand and could see that two fingers on his left hand were almost severed. We couldn't make out any other stab wounds, it looked like she hit bull's-eye in one shot.

Terry told us to leave him and don't touch anything he beckoned us outside. Tamina was sat on the steps leading to the next floor, she was still sobbing her chest rising and falling with each sob, the embroidered flowers on either side dancing with every heave it was sort of hypnotic and I had to catch myself from staring at the heaving of her chest, now was not the time.

"Look you guys its best you leave now don't want you guys around when the Police arrive, that will certainly look suspicious."

We both agreed told Tamina to stay strong and listen to Terry, we told Terry not to do anything stupid and to call us later to let us know what is going on. We walked off towards the tube station. Neither of us spoke we were trying to take in the scene that we had just left and understand what had just taken place. I was worried for Terry in case he got himself into something. I also thought what Tamina's option would be now. My phone rang it was Terry he wanted me to text him the name and number of a good defence solicitor, because he had just phoned the police and they were sure to arrest Tamina. I told him that I will talk with someone now and text him their number.

At home I spoke to a friend who I had worked with when I was a defence solicitor. I described the scene and gave him Terry's number. I was sure that he would help, he was a partner in one of East London's better crime firms, he had a good reputation for going the whole nine mile for his clients and certainly had some good results over the years. I had not come up against him at court, but had seen him in action where he had ripped into one of my prosecuting colleagues and destroyed the evidence that they were relying on. He assured me that he would look after Tamina and would ring Terry straight away. Just in case I texted his name and number to Terry, then I waited for Terry to call or come round my house to let me know what was going on.

I tried to stay up and rang Terry's number a few times, but his phone was switched off. Jerry had called me a few times as well to ask if I had heard anything. We were both getting very worried but we resisted the temptation to go to the police station. I didn't fall asleep until five in the morning and then only slept fitfully. Nicolette woke me up, she knew something was wrong by the look on my face and my anxious glance at my phone to see if Terry had called, but he hadn't. I explained to her what had happened last night and the death of Trendy. She told me things should be fine and that it sounded to her like self defence.

I heard our kids playing in the bathroom whilst they brushed their teeth. That was when it dawned on me, we did not see Tamina's child, where was he, a feeling of dread came over me, what if he had been somewhere in that room and hurt, we didn't see him but he could have been there. We hadn't heard him and in all the commotion of finding Trendy dead it had completed slipped my mind that her son should have been there as well. I had to speak with Terry, but I had to wait for him as I did not know where he was. I called Jerry and asked him if he had heard or seen Tamina's son last night, he swore and said he had forgotten about him, it didn't enter his head that the boy would be there. Maybe he was with a minder; we both prayed that this was the case.

I had to go to work, I had a busy schedule, in court all day one trial in the afternoon and a morning of sentence hearings. Perversely I was glad because I would be very busy and the day should go quickly then I could try and catch up with Terry in the afternoon. I could not keep my phone on in Court but made sure I turned it on during the lunch break. As soon as I turned it on it started beeping four missed calls from Jerry and two messages from Terry. I deleted Jerry's missed calls and went straight to Terry's messages.

"Home now, will call later need some sleep", and then later in the morning.

"Need to speak properly meet at bar 5pm. Your mate was brill!"

I breathed a sigh of relief, seemed things were okay. I rang Jerry he received the same texts, he sounded relived as well. Then I heard the tannoy calling my trial on, it was early, but I wasn't surprised. I hadn't done much preparation for the trial but it was simple enough. A common assault; all he said, she said, he did, I didn't, real stuff of nonsense which shouldn't have got to this stage. She was upset with him because he had spent some of the housekeeping money on drugs then stayed out all night sharing the drugs with friends, she's stuck at home with the kids wanting something to make her forget hoping he'd come home with some for her, he didn't, he came home high as a kite and nothing left for her. She threw the bottle steriliser at him and he slapped her, they struggled. Whilst struggling neighbours call the police and he's arrested. They were still arguing in court, he was pissed off because he spent a day in the cells then had to sleep at a friends' house. She was pissed because he wouldn't break his bail conditions and come round to see her or the kids even though she was broke and needed to get some essentials. He was found guilty and sentenced to one day in prison, deemed served, £20 fine and £20 costs.

I gathered my papers nodded to the bench, shook the defence lawyers hand and left court. On leaving court I spotted the couple walking hand in hand down the High Street, every few steps stopping to kiss each other passionately. I dumped my papers back at the office then rushed home to change and meet up with Terry. On arriving at the bar Jerry and Terry were already there, they had my favourite drink waiting for me. Even before I sat down I was asking Terry what had happened. Jerry and I sat enthralled as Terry spoke.

After we left he had managed to calm Tamina down long enough to get her to tell him what had happened. Trendy had contacted her the day before apologising for not having been in contact, he wanted to see his son and his mum enjoyed her time with him so much the last time she wanted to see him again. He persuaded her to let him take him promising not to do anything as he had learned his lesson. In order to placate her he said that he would bring his mother with him, she could collect the boy then he would leave. She agreed with his mother that she could take the boy and that he could stay over that night, the boy seemed happy to see her so she packed an overnight bag and said her goodbyes. She told me that the mother was very pleasant and polite so she suspected nothing, she had given Tamina her contact numbers and her address. Trendy left with his mother, they were to bring him back in the morning, it was her day off so there was no mad rush, but she wanted to go to Ilford to buy some clothes for him.

In the morning around ten thirty there was a knock on her door, she assumed it was Trendy and his mother returning with her son. As soon as she had opened the door Trendy pushed his way past her grabbed her by the throat and thrown her down to the floor. He jumped on top of her and started punching and slapping her, shouting at her "Who's the man!" over and over again he dragged her into the lounge and raped her on the floor.

He then took her keys from her bag and bolted the front door, he then phoned his mother and told her that Tamina said it would be okay to keep the boy until tomorrow. He then ordered her to make him some food, which she did. He followed her into the kitchen and threw the sharp knives out the window. He was watching her the whole time apart from when he went to the toilet, with the door open in case she tried to make a run for the front door or something. This gave her an opportunity. She had noticed that he had missed one of the knives which was in the sink; she had used it earlier to cut some bread so she hid it on top of the fridge freezer out of sight.

He was so cock sure of himself that he did not get dressed and lounged around in his boxer shorts. He continued to verbally and physically abuse her throughout the day. He was laughing at her calling her all sorts of names. As the day moved on he got angrier and angrier and she knew that she would have to do something drastic to get away from him. He was angry about being told what to do, she had asked him what he meant, but he kept saying to her;

"You know what I mean, those bastards think they can tell me what I can and cannot do, let them come again. This is me Trendy, I like doing this, I'm a man!"

She knew what he meant because Terry had hinted to her about the 'concerned citizens' but she tried to convince him that she didn't, she wanted to get him to talk about it as maybe that would calm him down and get the hell away from her. He finally opened up and described his ordeal with the masked men. He showed her the wound on his head and the bruising they had inflicted and how they called him a deviant and that he was perverted. He asked her what they meant; he denied being perverted and told her that he knew she liked sex with him since she liked it rough. He told her that she loved what he was doing to her now. She tried to console him, whilst thinking of a way out, but he pushed her away.

Time moved until almost five o'clock, he was a lot calmer and she thought that she could persuade him to go now. Then her phone rang, he told her to answer it, it was Raymond her new boyfriend, she got him off the phone quickly, but he knew it was another man and went into a rage. He started smashing up the furniture, he ripped up the cushions and screamed at her that she couldn't have another man because he wouldn't allow it; she was his to do with what he wanted. He slapped and punched her again and started to strangle her, he called her a slag, that no one else could have her, she was dirty because she had been with someone else, too dirty to live. She fought back, she managed to get away from him and ran to the kitchen he was close behind her. She grabbed anything she could get her hands on threw plates, bowls dishes forks, spoons cups and saucers at him, but still he kept coming towards her. She remembered the knife on top of the fridge freezer and tried to reach it, he was very close now, he made a grab at her and slipped over, she kicked him as hard as she could catching him in the chest, as he fell he aimed a kick at her missed her and put his bare foot through the glass washing machine door.

This gave her time to reach the knife, in the time it took her to get the knife he had got up and made another grab for her she had spun around at the same time making slashing moves with the knife, she caught him on his hand and arms. He tried to grab the knife but she was frantically flailing the knife, then she steadied herself and plunge the knife as hard as she could into him. He stood still for a moment, looked down at the knife then looked at her, blood was pouring from the wound. He called her a fucking bitch and slumped down onto the floor beside the washing machine.

She couldn't remember how long she had stood there looking at him, she felt frozen in time. She listened to him making little rasping noises, then a gurgle and then nothing, she knew he was gone. Then the tears started from deep inside her they welled up and then poured out, she couldn't control herself, her body functions went awry. She managed to control herself enough to get out of the kitchen; she ran to the lounge and found her phone that was when she rang Terry. After calling Terry she couldn't stay inside the flat knowing he was there and waited for Terry outside, the rest we know.

"What happened after we left with the police and everything?"

Once she had finished Terry told her that he had to call the police, but for her not worry as he will be with her every step of the way. He also explained that he would call me to get a good lawyer down to assist her. He thanked me for that, saying that the lawyer was top notched really knew his stuff and wouldn't stand for any nonsense from the police.

When the police came they separated him and Tamina and started to question them about what had happened even before they had entered the flat. Terry was telling them to go inside the flat and see what happened it will tell them all they needed to know, but they insisted on questioning them first. In the end Terry told them that he wasn't answering anymore questions that they should stop questioning Tamina and go inside the flat and make up their own minds. Two officers remained outside with them whilst the other four entered the flat. Within five minutes one of them came running out and proceeded to vomit all over the grassed gardens at the front of the block of flats, the other three came out ashen faced. One, who seemed to be the officer in charged radioed for CID and scene of crimes to attend, he then indicated to the others who were standing with Terry and Tamina to take them to the station. By this time Tamina had given Terry the contact number for Trendy's mother and urged him to make sure her son was safe.

At the station Terry was told to wait outside in the waiting area whilst they took Tamina inside. Terry had then spoken with my friend and he was on his way down. Terry heard him on the phone to the desk Sergeant and it seemed that he was laying the law down. A short time later one of the officers who had attended the scene took Terry through to an interview room where a CID officer was waiting to question him. Terry told them of the phone call from Tamina, he did not tell them about us or that he had entered the flat. He told them that he had gone to see her because she sounded troubled on the phone and when he got there all he could get out of her was that Trendy was dead and nothing else. They thanked him for his time and told him that he could go, he refused, and he told them that he would rather wait at the station for Tamina and that they should let her know that he was there.

He met the lawyer in the waiting area and greeted him, he promised to keep him informed about what was going on, and told him not to worry because he didn't think they could keep her there. He was called in shortly after, it was about eleven o'clock and it wasn't until four o'clock that the lawyer came out to let Terry know what was going on. He told Terry that they had started out to get her to confess to luring Trendy to her house in order to kill him because he had two timed her, but the more they checked out her story the more they realised that she was telling the truth. Her kitchen knives where out the window, only his fingerprints were on the broken furniture, the keys to her door had his fingerprints all over them, the fact that he was only in his boxer shorts, her cuts and bruises, the state of the kitchen, and his broken toe from smashing the washing machine. They were now more sympathetic and were offering them cups of tea and concerned that she needed to rest, but she wanted to continue. The break was to seek CPS advice about charging, he told Terry this could take one minute or many hours. Then they called him back in.

They didn't come out again until Seven thirty, the lawyer explained that CPS advice initially was to carry out further examination of the scene and then to ask Tamina further questions. Once this was done the further advice was to bail her to come back another day once all the investigations had been completed, they did intimate that they were thinking seriously about a manslaughter charge, but that he did not think that it would stick. Terry asked me what I thought, I told him in my view I wouldn't prosecute everything points to self defence, not many of my guys would want this one especially going before a jury who would definitely have sympathy for Tamina, I was certain that they would drop it.

They let her go and bailed her at about eight o'clock, Terry took her to his place to let her sleep, but she wanted to go straight to Trendy's mothers house to get her son. Then he described to us what he thought was the weirdest thing. The police had already informed Trendy's mother of what had happened, so she looked surprised when she saw Tamina. But then she hugged her and invited them both inside. Tamina ran to her son and hugged him long and hard, she began to cry again and started to say sorry to Trendy's mum, who brushed it away and said to Tamina that if it wasn't her it would have been someone else, she then told them all about her son and how he had even hit her, stolen her money and forced her to take care of children whilst he did who knows what to the children's mothers. She asked Tamina to stay with her as she could not go back to her flat and she had room that she would look after her. To his surprise Tamina agreed and that is where he left her. He has rung her a few times and she sounded happy and safe enough.

"Listen man, who knows what some people do. You was right Barry this guy was never gonna change maybe we should have killed him when we had the chance. I tell you now dat girl wouldn't have gone through all that if we had just snuffed his lights out there and then."

"You is right man, I knew in my blood when we had him that I wanted to kill it, dat ting didn't deserve to be alive and boddering people like dat. But again if we had left him would he have gone to Tamina and did her like dat so she had to kill him, I don't know man, all this has been going through my head all night. I don't know if you is right Jerry or Barry is right and we should'a left him be. But dat form a man I don't know he deserved to die but is it better it was through Tamina or would it be better if it was us, three masked men, I don't know?"

ROBERT KELLY chapter 12

The whole Trendy killing had affected Terry probably even more than he would let on to Jerry and I. For the next week he was very distant and seemed locked in his thoughts, but he would not share them. We all knew what he was wrestling with, I think we were all wrestling with the same thing, but we had to leave him to sort them out in his own way. He seemed to cheer up when Tamina confirmed to him that she had heard from the Police and they had confirmed they accepted her story of self defence and would not charge her. Apparently since his death three other Women including his mother had given statements confirming his violent tendencies and that they had been held captive by him in similar circumstances.

The press had a field day recounting stories about his sadistic sexual nature and called him 'The Predator'. However, once it was confirmed that no action was going to be taken against his killer press interest began to die down. Tamina was protected by anonymity, so they could not name her, but they did have pictures of her with her face faded out, if you knew her you would know that was her in the picture.

I managed to cheer Terry up some more when I confirmed that I had identified our next target a burglar named Robert Kelly. As he had the same name as the popular singer he called himself 'R', however he looked nothing like the singer. He was a short and skinny fair skinned black man; he had a large forehead covered in acne scars, with a small upturned nose, which seemed to be continuously running with snot on account of his excessive over use of Cocaine. He always looked scruffily dressed even though most of his clothes sported the latest designer labels. He was always dressed in white trainers, the baggiest of blue jeans and a hooded sweatshirt, in the summer he would swap the hooded sweatshirt for a tee shirt and baseball cap finished off with Ray Ban sunglasses. He kept his hair cut short always getting a number one on his frequent visits to the barbers.

He was a burglar and a particularly nasty one, having spent time in young offenders' institutes for aggravated burglary. He had broken into the home of an elderly couple but was disturbed by the old man, rather than running out he took delight in beating the old man up, fracturing his eye socket and cracking one of his ribs. He was caught when he was stopped by police that same night because he fitted the description given. When they stopped him and whilst questioning him about his whereabouts they noticed blood on his trainer's forensics proved it to be the old man's blood.

He had come to my attention whilst I was prosecuting one of his friends for burglary, his name had come up as one of the group that this guy moved around with and he had implicated him in some of the burglaries. His 'friend' alleged that he was the ring leader and would pick the jobs for them to do, but no charges were brought against him, because apart from the statement nothing could be proved.

A few weeks later he was arrested and charged for a burglary at an old peoples home, he had gone from room to room threatening the residents and stealing whatever he could, money, jewellery credit cards. He was caught trying to sneak out a window which he hadn't realised was alarmed. The nurse, who was sleeping throughout the robberies, woke up and confronted him and started hitting him with a broom handle as he tried to squeeze out the window. The other nurse who was also asleep woke up and called the police.

He was charged and appeared in court where I was prosecuting him. I noticed early on that there was a problem with the charge. On his arrest they could not find any of the stolen goods on him, so he must have had an accomplice, none of the statements taken from the victims mentioned a second person, nor could any of them identify him during an identification parade. The only link they had was that he was caught by the nurses climbing through the window. That wasn't a problem in itself because the law was pretty clear he was found on the premises, where he should not have been, and robberies had taken place, he was, at the least, guilty of being found on enclosed premises.

The real problem was his story of how he got there; it was totally unbelievable yet believable. He said that he was walking past the Home on his way to his girlfriend's house, she lived around the corner, when he saw a young black guy about six feet tall climb through the window and run off down the road. He hadn't heard any alarm so worried for the old folks inside the home went to the window to see if he could help anyone.

On looking through the window he couldn't see anyone and was surprised because if someone had broken in some of the old folks or at the least one of the nurses would be in the corridor. So he decided to climb in through the window in order to locate one of the nurses and tell them what he found. When asked why he didn't simply ring the front door bell, he replied that he didn't think of that. On climbing through the window the alarm went off, which surprised him and scared him so he decided to climb back out in case they blamed him for whatever it was that the other guy had done and that was when the nurse started beating him with the stick. I could see problem written all over this one and made the early decision this was not a case for me, but that I would watch what went on.

In court he entered not guilty pleas, he had only been charged with burglary so I made an application for a second charge of 'being found on enclosed premises' to be added. Of course the defence lawyer objected and it was left that the reviewing lawyer would consider the point and make a written application to the court. I found out later that this was not done, although the prosecutor doing the trial tried to make a plea bargain to Kelly's lawyer to accept that as a lesser plea and they would drop the burglary charge. It was too late and eventually the prosecutor decided to drop the case before the trial started. He walked free with a smirk on his face, bounced out of court with his posse. I saw them later on in a pub celebrating.

On meeting up with Jerry and Terry I had described R Kelly to them and explained why I had targeted him for us, we all agreed that he would be the next target. Jerry seemed particularly pleased and said that he couldn't wait to get back to the 'tool table' and sort out some low life. Terry just asked if we were going to do this one right. Jerry looked at me; we both knew what he was referring to.

"Listen man, we did the last one right, in fact there was no right or wrong. As I said before it was probably better he was snuffed by one of his women, no one would have known what he was about if his body just turned up on the street somewhere, he would have been just another victim. At least this way there is no doubt about what he was, you understand me?"

"Yeah, I know all dat man, I've been over it a hundred times and I know but did it have to be her?"

"Yeah I think it did, she was his first real love and all that, and she's strong man, she's bloody strong I doubt if any of the other women he had would have been able to handle it, so yeah it probably did!"

"Is sense you talking man, you know she's back at work no change in the way she deal with people. We have our little sessions with her, but she gonna make it. You know she still see his mother and they talk and talk for hours on end, seems like dis woman is the mother she never had, strange tings man!"

"What about this guy, when we going to do it?"

I explained that I had just started following him around and I hadn't got the full low down on his hang outs and things yet, but if they give me another few days I would have sorted it all out. Terry then interjected and told us that he knows him as he sometimes comes down to the youth centre.

"Yeah, he's a cocky little runt always pulling out wads of money trying to impress the others in the centre, always hustling at the pool table or sitting in the corner gambling, always with about three or four other guys just as shallow as he is, he always comes across to me as the ring leader, always looks like they're plotting something or other. I don't like him had to kick him out on occasion when he has just got too much, I don't think he likes me either, I can tell you tings about him."

He then told us his usual hang outs, the days he's at the centre. The problem we had was that he was always with someone, Terry could never remember a time when he was alone, he seemed the sort of guy that needed company in order to feel big. We had to devise a way of getting him on his own, or get the others he was with to back off giving us sufficient time to get him into the back of the van. This was going to be difficult, but we had to work it out. We decided that we needed to observe him in order to see if there was 'a chink in his armour' as Jerry had said. Terry had confirmed that he would be at the centre tomorrow night as he was usual there on a Wednesday evening, sitting in the corner with his cronies plotting or planning something, whilst playing cards. He would watch him and report back to us if there was a way.

Jerry had to leave early as usual he was on a promise with someone somewhere and he was going home to spruce up and have a little work out to ensure that his muscles were as toned as possible. Terry and I continued talking, I wanted to press him more about his thinking on Tamina and Trendy, but I didn't. I knew that he would clam up and that we would end up sitting in silence, so I left him to it, but I did tell him what I thought. I started by telling him it was like Jerry had said many weeks ago, a juxtaposition, we were damned by circumstance if we didn't finish him off and damned by circumstances if we did. As we had said before, we could beat him as much as possible but all that sadism was in his genes, they made him what he was and that unless we were geneticists we couldn't change him.

I told Terry that I thought Jerry had the right idea about all this; the problem with us was that we thought too deeply about things and we let them bother us. I asked him where Jerry was now; he was out having fun and waiting for the next target. Whereas, we were here in the bar caressing our drinks, and wandering through the morality of it all. I told him that I thought that if we picked the right targets we would not have to worry about morality, it would just be right, we would have right on our side.

"Yeah but, whatever the rights or wrongs of it, what keeps, running around in my head is what you said when we did Trendy and Jerry and me was gonna top him, because of that we eased up on him, and then it had to be Tamina who had to do our job. We had him. But you was right man, that wasn't what we signed up for and maybe we shouldn't have done him. I dunno!"

We carried on talking for a while longer, I managed to get him onto the subject of Robert Kelly, told him Trendy was history now we had to move on, it seemed like Tamina had, so we had to put it down to experience and move on as well. We talked about R Kelly, as we began to call him, and simultaneously we started to sing R Kelly's you remind me of my car, which brought a smile to Terry's face. I said that it would be quite funny that when we got him he broke out into an R Kelly song.

We called it a night and went on our different ways home. On the way home, at the top of my road I noticed a group of young guys hanging around, I didn't think anything of it as this was quite normal for this area, they never did anything much just hung around, met up then went on to wherever it was that they were going to. My attention was drawn to them as I hadn't seen this particular bunch around this area before, but there did seem to be a familiar face amongst them. They were laughing and talking loudly and I knew that because of this, any time soon police will be arriving as one of the residents would have called them. The local youth know not to make too much noise in this area as the neighbourhood watch here was very active. As I walked past them the familiar face became very familiar, it was R Kelly, I was so surprised that I stopped and stared at him, he didn't notice but one of his group did.

"Is wha'ppen man, you know we?"

I shook my head and tried to hurry up past them, but the same guy who spoke came up beside me.

"You look like you lost bruv, you want me to escort you home?"

I told him to get lost and to do one before he started something he couldn't end. I tensed up and my shoulders hunch a bit more bracing myself for whatever was going to come next. I was expecting a fight and readied myself for the first blow, but it never came. He was now right by my side as I had stopped and I looked him in the eye. He was smaller than me in build and shorter also; he looked me up and down and then looked over to his friends who were now about fifteen yards further back. His faced went slightly ashen as he realised how far away he was from his group and that if I started swinging he would get hurt long before the rest of his group could catch up with me.

I said to him that he had better go back to his boys as it looked like he was missing them. He backed away from me but the wrong way I was now between him and his friends, but I simply eased him out the way and told him in my strongest Jamaican patois to "Gallang lickle bwoy!" he simply walked back to his friends, who were by now laughing at him and goading him. I carried on walking home, but thought I didn't want to lead them to my house so went left instead of right and doubled back on myself, checking all the time to see if they were following me, they were not.

On reaching home I sat on the doorstep for a while waiting to see if, just in case, they had followed me, no-one passed. I was thinking about the irony of it, how we had just been talking about R Kelly and there he was right in front of me. It struck me that this was reinforcement, a message from above that what we were doing and planning to do was the right path. I would also ordinarily not be so antagonistic when there was a group of young men likely to confront me, I heard and read the stories of people being kicked to hell and even killed for simply confronting a group of people, and there I was right in the thick of a group of young men. However, I was not afraid as something told me they would not and could not do anything to me, that I had the power and one of their group was going to feel our force anytime soon.

A few days later Terry and I met up, Jerry was out wining and dining a new client. He wouldn't tell us who it was just that it was one of the top premiership football players who was looking for a change of Agents and had heard about his work from others in his team. Terry had some news on R Kelly, apparently he lived just behind the community centre where Terry worked, with his parents who did not like his friends so they were not allowed anywhere near his home. His Father was a strict disciplinarian who thought nothing of dishing out punishment if any of his children disobeyed him. He and R Kelly had many run-ins because he did not like his lifestyle, but allowed him to remain in his house so that he could, at least have some control over him. He was short like R Kelly but was a bigger build and wasn't afraid to throw his weight around his home to keep order and try to keep his son on the straight and narrow. He knew he was failing, but this made him more determined.

This meant that we had two windows of opportunity to get hold of him, when he was leaving his house and on his way home. We discussed both options and decided we had to try and get him when he was leaving his house, which he did not do until late in the evening. Because his Father was so strict, if he was not home by midnight he would lock the doors and R would have to find somewhere to stay. This meant that he would be running the streets all night and therefore difficult to get on his own.

Terry had confirmed that he would meet up with his 'posse' at the community centre on Wednesdays and Fridays around eight o'clock, which meant our window of opportunity would be just before when he would more than likely be on his own, which would be walking from his home to the centre. It was Tuesday and as Jerry wasn't around Terry and I planned for events to take place on the Friday. Terry was to set things in motion and I would let Jerry know the plan, date and time. With the plan in motion the high I felt when we were planning for Johnson Cole came back. I couldn't wait for Friday to come around so that we could get back to action getting rid of another bad egg from our streets. It was going to be easy.

The days flew by and before I knew it Friday had come. I just had to get through court and then it would be time for action. Court was unusually quiet not much was going on, which meant that the day dragged on. All the usually recidivists were there either in packs or on their own. Some looked hung over; some looked high on drugs, other just coming down from their high the night before. Some looked pensive, others looked surly and confident that nothing could touch them, that they have been here before and all they were going to get was a slap on the wrists. The magistrates were even more lenient than normal and from the court rooms you could hear triumphant shouts from the recidivists being told that they were free to go, pay five pounds a week, see a probation officer, get treatment for your habit and so on.

There was a buzz in the waiting areas as people met up talking about why they were in court, how badly they were treated by John Bull, what they were doing tonight, where they could get a hit for the weekend. Men were chatting up women, women chatting up men, someone had a ghetto blaster blaring away on high, before security told him to turn it off otherwise it would be confiscated, others had their mobile phones and their I Pods playing music, the tinny sounds coming out of their headphones mingled, making one feel like they were suffering from Tinnitus. The court house felt like one big social club, the security guards had a busy day running from one group to another ordering, imploring them to turn off their phones and their I Pods, or to stop eating and drinking, to stop arguing. The punishment, confiscation or ejection, no one took them seriously, everything was turned off then by the time they had turned their backs to approach the next person they were turned on again.

I just had to get through the afternoon list, get back to the office then home, eat, change and meet up with Terry and Jerry. I was thinking about nothing in particular, simply getting ready for a simple plea on a shoplifting matter, when I heard a commotion by the main doors. A group of about four young guys were arguing with security, I could overhear some of it. It seems that they had taken umbrage at being told they had to be searched and to empty their pockets before going through the metal detectors. More security guards turned up and refused entry to the 'posse' until they gave in to being searched. I'm not sure whether it was the carnival like atmosphere in the main waiting area or the size and number of security guards, but they all soon submitted to being searched, still abusing the security guards for doing their job.

They entered the main area; this was when I noticed that it was R Kelly and the same 'Posse' from the other night. They bounced into the court house and gathered by a bench occupied by an older couple who looked like they were waiting for a sibling to finish in court. They were quickly made to feel uncomfortable by the 'posse' who were talking loudly and staring directly at them. R Kelly had his mobile phone blaring a tinny sounding tune, a security guard looked over at them, but noting the earlier hassles with them decided to let this one go. The older couple soon moved to a more peaceful area of the court house. The one I had the confrontation with the other night caught my eye, he seemed to recognise me as he was staring hard at me, he said something to R Kelly, they both laughed then turned back to the main group and continued to laugh and joke and poke fun at the by now harassed security staff. It seemed that the party got bigger with their entrance and no one was going to stop the fun.

I spoke with a list officer who confirmed that it was the one I had the confrontation with who was up on a shoplifting charge. I sought out my colleague who was to prosecute and made a swap with him. I definitely wanted the pleasure of being opposite this guy in court. I went through the papers given to me to get a flavour of the type of villain I had been confronted by the other night.

I read that he had been caught in Sainsbury's stealing ten pounds worth of meat; apparently he was seen by a security guard stuffing the lamb chops, and lamb mince down his 'very' baggy trousers and only paying for a tin of corned beef. On leaving the store he was stopped by two guards, who expecting a fight had put on stab proof vests, but on confronting him he came with them meekly and was apologising even before he had got back into the store, pulling the meat from his trousers and imploring them to let him go.

In court we settled down to the proceedings, I shook hands with the defence lawyer and nodded to the bench. I could hear his little 'posse' behind me in the gallery; they were talking loudly and generally being offensive about myself, the clerk to the court and the bench. I was a slave doing the white man's bidding, looking to lock up one of my own, The bench were Teletubbies with their different coloured faces and fat faces, the clerk was Ebenezer Scrooge, bent over his desk like he was counting out his money.

They didn't even try to be discreet, so much so that the Chairman of the Bench ordered them to be cleared out of his court, before you could blink security guards had converged on them from all sides and were physically herding them out of the court room. The commotion continued for a while outside then died down. I could see this guy physically shrink after his fan club was ejected. The Chair of the Bench asked what his plea was, and to the surprise of his lawyer he meekly replied "Guilty". It looked as if, with his 'posse' around him he was going to tough it out and plead not guilty but with them gone, he reverted to his cowardly self.

As he entered guilty pleas the hearing was adjourned for what is known as an all options report, and the Chair of the Bench said that custody was a serious consideration for him noting his previous convictions for theft and burglary. He went away meekly to locate his 'posse' and spin them tall stories of how he "did tell dem mens dem dat dey can't touch him and nuttin' dey can do to him" and how he told me "You ain't nuttin' man hiding behind dem mans dem…" and his 'posse' would laugh and slap him on the back and agree with him, he was "dread man, dem mans is butters, so when's your trial?" I had a wry smile as I left the court room wondering how he was going to answer that question, no doubt, he will blame his lawyer who told him to plead early and all he will get is a fine, whereas, if he went to trial he could get all sorts of punishments, "So I done what de expert say innit?"

Buoyed by what had happened in court, the rest of the day flew past and it was now soon time to become the regulator of a troublesome little man who needed fixing in our unique and special way. I did start to think that it was a shame that it wasn't this guy; he was such a coward that it would have been so easy.

The plan for the evening was that we would meet Terry at the Centre then change in the van. Terry would then drive us towards R Kelly's house; we would wait for him at the top of his road. We had to be quick as at that time of the evening his road became a popular cat run for drivers trying to miss the heavy traffic on the high road. Unfortunately, Jerry was late, we had planned to meet up by seven o'clock, this would give us time to change and get to R Kelly's road by seven thirty, which would give us some waiting time as he would normally leave his house between seven thirty and eight o'clock. Terry and I were just about to abort the operation when Jerry showed up, very apologetic and complaining about the traffic and some client wanting a last minute massaging of their ego before they signed a contract with him.

It was now seven forty and we had to hurry, but first Terry checked to see if R Kelly was already at the centre. He came back pretty quickly to confirm that some of his 'posse' were there but he had not arrived yet. This meant that we had to hurry as he could already be on his way and if he was we had missed our chance to get him. Terry was angry because he didn't want to be rushing as things could go wrong. He felt that we should abort the mission and leave it for another day, Jerry and I were of the view that we should get ready and get round to his Road, if he had already left then so be it, we leave it for another day. If he hadn't then nothing lost and we get our man.

We changed in the van and set off to try and intercept R Kelly. I squeezed into the middle seat with Jerry on my left, he had wound the window down, the breeze was blowing his fake locks into his face, which seemed to annoy him as he took off his hat and laid them into his lap. As we got to the top of his road Terry nudged me and pointed to a small figure walking huddled up against the cold wind, it was him. Terry swung the van into a three point turn and went back to the top of the road, he let two cars pass him then swung the van into the last parking space at the very top of the road. Jerry and I jumped out of the van and ran around to the back and opened the doors. As R Kelly approached we pretended to be arguing about something in the back of the van. I had hold of the tape and Jerry had the sack ready.

Jerry and I then pretended to fight pushing and shoving each other. Jerry pushed me into R Kelly just as he stopped to watch the rasta and his dry head friend fight over the contents of the bag. As I knocked into him I turned around quickly and grabbed him around his waist and swung him into Jerry who in one quick movement managed to throw the sack over his head. I still had hold of him and let go once the sack was completely over him, I then taped him up and Jerry and I lifted him up and threw him into the back of the van. We quickly jumped in after him and Terry ran to the back and slammed shut the back doors. Jerry gave me a high five and slapped me on my thigh, he was laughing loudly, a kind of guffaw. I smiled at him and slapped him back, then gave him another high five. It was so exhilarating when a plan came together, especially how we had to improvise in order for it to go smoothly.

I was sitting back revelling in the acting job we had pulled off and had completely forgotten about R Kelly, until I heard a grunt from underneath the sack in the middle of the floor of the van. Jerry and I looked at each other and laughed, then Jerry kicked him too see if he was still with us. He let out a scream then said in a quiet lisping choirboy type voice,

"Hey man, can we talk about this, I'm sure if we talk we can come to some kind of understanding, what you say guys hey?"

Jerry gave him a hard kick to his shin and told him to shut up and to save his breath as we were not listening to him. He let out a sigh, then we heard the sound of water running, or at least, we thought it was water.

"You raas you've pissed yourself and we ain't even done nothing to you yet!"

I tried hard to suppress the laughter that was welling up inside me, but I couldn't. My sides hurt from laughing so much Terry started banging on the side of the van to get me to be quiet, but it was no good I couldn't stop. Terry turned up the sound on the radio to try and drown out my laughter, "This ain't nothing but the real thing baby..."

We pulled up outside the Torture Chamber just as I finished laughing. I heard the engine and the radio turn off simultaneously, then Terry coming round to the back of the van, he opened the door and looked at me with daggers in his eyes.

"You nearly got us stopped by de man dem, I was banging on de side to get you to shut up cos dey was on our tail. I had to turn up the music and try and ignore dem, what the raas was so funny anyway?"

I pointed to the pool of urine surrounding the prone body of R Kelly, apart from the occasional sigh it was if he was a mannequin waiting to be dressed for a shop window.

"Oh my raas, is he still alive, de raas bwoy piss himself even before we do anyt'ing to him, he certainly ain't like his namesake, you two better get him inside!"

"Listen, which two I ain't touching dat, he soaked right through, seeing as he nearly got us caught he can do it." And then he pointed at me.

I couldn't argue my funny bone was still playing up and looking at the expression on Terry's face nearly started me off again. I let them go ahead of me as I pulled him out of the van and threw him over my shoulder. I could feel his discharge, which had soaked even the sack covering him and was now soaking into my shoulder. I was sure it had begun to drip down my back as well. The smell was awful, like cat's piss in one of those litter trays. I hurried into the chamber and literally threw him down into the chair. Terry quickly tied him up, hands tethered by his side, ankles to the chair leg. Jerry was already by the tool table and was sorting out which tools to use. Terry and I stood either side of R Kelly; he sat with his head down sighing every now and then and reeking of urine.

He could hear the clanking of the tools as Jerry began picking out his favourite and he could feel the presence of Terry and I either side of him. He made a loud gulping sound and began to shake his head, then his whole body began to tremble, he gulped some more then let out a loud fart. Terry looked at me and I looked at Terry, it took all I had not to lose control again. It didn't take long; Jerry had heard the fart over the commotion of the clanking tools and shouted out,

"Oh my God is he still there or has he exploded?"

I lost it, next thing I knew I was on the floor holding my sides to stop them from splitting. Terry was laughing as well, but he was more in control and was beckoning to me to get up.

"Come on man, hah! Hah! you need to be serious, this hee ha, is serious, get up man, please!"

I tried to compose myself and had managed to pull myself up. Both my hands were resting on the table supporting the rest of my body. I looked at R Kelly sweat was dripping from his brow and he was trembling, he did not say anything, he didn't need to his eyes told us all we needed to know, he was terrified. For a while I wasn't sure if he was terrified of us or terrified of the evil smell emanating from his buttocks. In order to bring me back into serious mode Terry leaned over and punched me hard on the arm and told me to pull myself together, which did the trick.

"Now can we get on with what we came here for, this fart arse bwoy!"

Terry then leaned over and smacked R Kelly around the face. With that he let out another loud farting noise and sighed loudly. That wasn't the response that Terry expected and he just exploded into fits of laughter. It was my turn to try and compose Terry, I looked at him with laughing eyes to be more serious, but it just made him worse. He beckoned me to have a go at him. I smacked him on his left cheek again he farted loudly, and sighed. He looked up at me not saying a word but his eyes were begging me to stop, he had had enough and we hadn't even got started yet. Jerry came over and dropped his selected weaponry onto the table, R Kelly's eyes popped and he sighed again. Jerry looked at me then at Terry then back at me.

"Listen, I hope you're having fun, it my turn now!"

He picked up a large mallet, held it out in front of him as if examining it, then made some practice swipes smashing it onto an imaginary skull. He smiled and walked over to R Kelly where he held the mallet inches from his face then raised it as if to smash him on the top of his head. R Kelly sighed loudly and then the unmistakeable sound of a number two, seconds later the smell of faeces filled the air.

"Lord have mercy, listen man the bastard's shit himself, bloody hell that smell bad man!" Jerry backed away sniffed the air then backed away some more to get away from the rancid smell.

It was too late for Terry and I we both hit the floor together laughing as hard as we could at the same time smelling the foul smell and almost retching, then laughing, then retching again. Terry looked at me and said,

"I ain't going near dat t'ing man fuck it smells bad, how we gonna get him out of here it's got to go in the van you talk to him quickly then let's get him out!"

I had a handkerchief in my back pocket which I quickly wrapped around my face like a Cowboy in a western travelling through a dust storm. I composed myself with the help of the smell of faeces filling up the torture chamber. Jerry had backed away to the main door and looked like he was getting ready for a quick getaway in case the smell got too bad for him. Terry remained on the floor convinced that the smell would go up and that fresher air was to be had the lower you got to the floor. I was on my own, it was my target so I had to get the message to him, but this time I had to do it as quickly as possible before I was overpowered by that awful smell.

I struggled over to R Kelly, from the corner of my eye I could see Terry crawling away towards Jerry and the door; he looked up at me and shouted for me to hurry up because he couldn't take the smell. I had to put my hand over my nose as well I told him who we were, that he had been a bad boy and we were here to make sure he thought again about the life he was leading. I told him that we were the defenders of the community and that we were here to protect the community from his type and if it meant meting out violence to those opposed to our community then we were here to do just that to him. Each time I spoke I had to take my hands from my nose so that he could understand me and hear the menace in my voice. But, each time I did this I gagged on the smell emanating from him. I wanted to hit him repeatedly but I didn't want to get too close to him in case I threw up and added to the already pungent atmosphere.

I asked him if he understood what I was saying to him, he nodded his head and sighed. I told him that if he did not understand then we would repeat this over and over again until he got the message. I was hoping and praying that he got the message first time, I wasn't sure that I could go through this again.

"Yeah man, hmm, I get it, I understand, I ain't gonna rob no houses no more, you can count on that. You won't have to worry about me, look at what I've done to meself, hmm. Don't hurt me man, please let me go home, please!?"

I was relieved he seemed to understand what we wanted from him. I told him that we were taking him back now and that we'd be watching him, mess up and he'd be back here with us and that the next time we wouldn't be so nice to him. He nodded and sighed again. I called over to Terry and Jerry to help me get him back into the van, but they both shook their heads.

"There ain't no way I'm touching him or getting anywhere near that stinking raas."

"Listen man you are on your own, just untie him and bring him to the van, we'll be waiting outside for you."

They left me to it, I untied him as quickly as possible, threw the sack over his head and told him to walk ahead of me to the van. I had one hand on his shoulder the other over my nose. He walked slowly stiff legged his butt cheeks clenched firmly, you could hear a squelching noise every step he made. On reaching the van I pushed him in and told him to lie still. Jerry slammed the doors shut and quickly ran to the front of the van leaving me in the back with the rancid odour of faeces, urine and sweat.

I sat in the corner holding my nose wishing that Terry would hurry to our destination so that I could get some fresh air. I heard the engine turn over and the music began to blare simultaneously, we were moving, I could hear Terry and Jerry laughing in the front of the van. I just prayed that we would reach our destination soon.

Thankfully it wasn't long before the van pulled over and the back doors swung open, the sweet smell of fresh air wafted into the van and I took huge gulps of it as if I was a new born baby taking my first breath. I shoved R Kelly out of the van and Jerry pulled off the sack pushed him and told him to get lost! He disappeared into the dark to make his own way home. I jumped out of the back of the van and leaned over the back wheel and vomited. I used the handkerchief to wipe my face and mouth. Jerry had stepped back, looked at me and shook his head, then laughing went back to the front seat of the van. I tried to get into the front but they both told me to get back into the back as they could still smell R Kelly on me. They drove me home.

NICOLETTE chapter 13

I rushed in throwing off my clothes and straight into the shower. I remained in the shower for at least thirty minutes emptying the bottle of shower gel in an attempt to get the stench of faeces, urine, sweat and vomit from my skin. Nicolette was waiting for me as I alighted from the shower. She had my discarded clothes, mask and all in her hand asking me what the problem was and what the attire was all about. I tried lying first telling her something about helping Terry paint one of the meeting rooms in the centre, but I could see she didn't believe me, maybe because of the lack of paint on the overalls, or maybe the fact that you did not need a mask to paint a wall.

She sniffed the overalls and recoiled asking me what the hell was shit and piss doing on my clothes if all I was doing was painting with Terry and Jerry. I lied again and spun a yarn about trying to fix a blocked toilet in the Centre and getting sprayed with sewage, which was why I couldn't wait to get into the shower and clean myself off. She gave me a withering look then left the bathroom smelly clothes in her hand. I heard her go downstairs mumbling to herself, I heard the washing machine start, then I heard Nicolette go back into the bedroom.

I really wanted to tell her there and then about our crusade to clean the streets. I wanted to tell her about Johnson Cole, the truth about Aaron Trendway and about Robert Kelly. But, I couldn't I thought I knew what her reaction would be and I wasn't ready for it just yet, we had only just started and I think after 'Trendy' we wanted to make sure ourselves that we were not simply vigilantes taking the law into our own hands. I wanted to tell her that if the law and the police couldn't do it then it was down to the community to make a stand, but that someone had to force the hand of the community and act as its lever. Someone needed to stand up and represent the needs and desires of the community and say on its behalf that "We are not going to take this crap from you bastards anymore!" Someone had to do what the community wanted but did not do either because it was not organised, or was scared or because it was indifferent to the plight of its own neighbours. Those concerned individuals bold enough to do something were Terry, Jerry and I, even if we hid our identities and cleaned up the streets by stealth. We knew that the community needed us, even if it did not ask us or even know of our existence, it damned well needed us and we were here to do its bidding.

I wasn't sure that Nicolette would understand or accept what we were doing. She had always been very firm in her views that the law would sort it out, eventually. It may be slow, that was because it was a large unwieldy mass, but that it would catch up with wrongdoers eventually and punish them accordingly. Her view was very idealistic and my view had sort of been polarised by my experiences on both sides of the criminal law fence. Maybe being a barrister she did not get so involved in the nitty gritty of the Law, dealing with the execution of the law and arguing a point in law that would ensure her client would achieve some crumb of success. This, I think, gave her a certain naivety about justice and how it was meted out by the court system.

We would argue for hours about sentences meted out to this or that person. I would be frustrated that it was not more; she would defend the decision and argue on the basis that the judgement was correct in law. I would argue that you could not just look blithely at the law book, but because we were dealing with real people, circumstances had to dictate the type of sentence. That the courts would only look at the circumstances of the defendant and almost always forgot about the circumstance of the victim and even the effect on the wider community.

Nicolette would argue that this was not the job of the law but was for government and the community itself to deal with and change laws accordingly. I couldn't agree with this as sometimes the law makers and the communities would be at odds, who would decide then. I always argued that it had to be a conglomerate of all involved to ensure that good decisions are made, that we could not just simply rely on the executive or rely on the courts to pass the right sentence and accept whatever decisions they made. We would argue like this for hours, even days bringing up examples to reinforce our point of view.

I remained in the shower for at least thirty minutes, simply letting the hot water run over me; I had used up a whole bottle of shower gel and now I just wanted to think and the hot running water let me do this. I had managed to develop two trains of thought, one was whether I should tell Nicolette and the other was about the events of the night, just thinking about R Kelly made me laugh out loud, but I would be brought immediately back to reality thinking about what Nicolette would say when I told her what it was that we were really doing. I made up my mind that I would not tell her, but I was never a good liar when it came to her, but what else was I to do?

I finished in the shower, dried myself off and put on my dressing gown as I walked out of the bathroom. I could hear the washing machine on its final spin cycle, and thought that at least the evidence had now been cleaned up. This made me think of R Kelly again and I imagined him standing in his shower trying to clean himself up, thinking about us and crapping himself again. I could hear his father banging on the bathroom door, shouting at him to hurry up and come out of the bathroom and asking him what that awful smell was.

I smiled rather than laugh out loud at this image, I didn't want to wake the kids. I entered the bedroom, Nicolette was still awake, she had this way of lying as still as possible when she wanted me to think she was asleep, not realising that she tossed and turned and made a low humming type noise when she was really asleep. I took off my dressing gown and got into bed, trying to sound very tired so we wouldn't get into the inevitable questioning about the state of my clothes and what I had been getting up to. If I went straight to sleep I wouldn't have to lie to her.

I couldn't sleep and I knew Nicolette wasn't sleeping, but I tried my best to pretend to sleep and hold off the inevitable questions. I could feel a warm glow emanating from her body, which made me feel warm, I turned over to snuggle up to her, she remained perfectly still. We lay like this for a good few minutes; she then turned over and kissed me, pushed me on my back and got on top of me. She pinned my arms to the mattress and looked me directly in the eye.

"I always know when you're lying to me, but I'm not going to press you on this I know you guys are up to something I've been talking with Eva and she says that she thinks the same, she also mentioned overalls and a mask. No doubt, when you are ready you will tell me. I know you will!"

I couldn't say anything apart from mumbling a sort of apology whilst still trying to maintain that the story I had given was the truth. I knew that there was no point in emphasising the point so I laid back and enjoyed my wife on top of me controlling the action from her lofty position. It was, as usual, great lovemaking and we were soon both finished and fell asleep intertwined. Nicolette fell asleep first I soon followed lulled to sleep by her breath blowing gently onto my face.

My phone was ringing, I turned over to look at the time, it was seven o'clock, Nicolette was already up and seeing to the children. I reached over to my phone, it was Terry, I answered, and as soon as I did all I could hear was fits of laughter. I started to laugh when I realised that he was laughing about the events of the previous night. Then, in between his laughter, started to hum an R Kelly song and then said 'oh shit!' I was now in stitches.

"Man that has got to be one of the funniest situations I have ever been in. The look on your face when you had to carry him to the van, what's that advert? Priceless! Have you got rid of his smell from you? You know, I almost don't care if he doesn't listen to us, just to bring him back in, oh man!"

Nicolette came to the door and looked at me trying to work out what was so funny. Her eyes questioned me, but I knew that I shouldn't say anything, I smiled at her and she went away. I told Terry that I would talk to him later, maybe meet up for a drink and a de-brief and asked him if he could get Jerry along as well, if he wasn't on another booty call. He rang off singing another R Kelly ditty. I lay in bed for a while thinking about R Kelly and whether we had frightened him off sufficiently, I also thought about telling Nicolette the truth and how she would take it. Before I knew it time had flown by and I had to hurry in case I was late for work, I resolved to find myself some time later in the day to think things through and probably talk them over with Terry and Jerry as well.

That evening we met up at the usual place Terry and Jerry were already there and they had my favourite tipple waiting for me. I sat down and took a swig of my drink, I looked at both of them and we all started laughing. I wondered aloud how R Kelly must be feeling now, Terry and Jerry both said simultaneously;

"Like shit!" Jerry then added "Listen as long as the smelly sod got the message who cares how he is feeling. I'm bloody annoyed cos I couldn't get to use any of the tools on him. Listen, I didn't know a man could smell that bad!"

"If dat was me I would be laying low for a whole month, I doubt I could face anyone after dat!"

We all laughed again, then Jerry started to mimic his sighing and making intermittent farting noises. He then pretended to be me holding him at arms length, holding my nose and frogmarching him to the van. "Funniest thing I ever saw!"

I managed to stifle my laughter long enough to tell Terry that Eva and Nicolette had been talking as they were worrying about what we were up to. Terry confessed that Eva had been asking him hard questions about what we had been getting up to and that he was that close to telling her the truth. He hadn't because he wasn't sure how she would take it, of course, she knew that he could handle himself, his time as a drug dealer taught him how to do that, but he was worried that if he told her she would fret about him going back into prison. He also worried if she would actually get the morality of what it was that they were doing. I told him what I had told Nicolette last night in case Eva questioned him and that I was fretting over the same thing.

"Listen, what if they agree with you, why haven't you looked at it like that, they're your wives, your companions they should support you and damn the other consequences. But I understand where you're coming from I'm having problems with Nelson still, if I told him what we're doing he'd probably look at me in a different light, but I ain't doing this to impress him and I'm sure you guys ain't doing this to impress your wives either?"

We both looked at him and nodded in agreement, I added that it wasn't about impressing, but my wife can be very high and mighty when it comes to the law and it's applications and of course, she'd be worried about what might happen to me, she's already said to me that I am not Terry and that I shouldn't try to be.

"What is dat suppose to mean?"

I explained to Terry that it was a compliment; she was saying that he could look after himself but I was just an egghead lawyer who was not street smart. Terry cast me a look to say 'she really doesn't know you does she?' I smiled at him and winked to say 'that's the way I want it!'

"Listen, guys another thing you don't seem to have considered, what if something did happen to one of you, God forbid you ending up in hospital, but how you gonna explain away a black eye, or a gash or a sprain or something. It's easy for me I ain't got no-one that close to go prying, but you guys have. Thinking it through, if I was you, I think I would make love hard and good and then for pillow talk when they is feeling all soft and bubbling tell them about the star chamber. You don't have to tell them everything but tell them how it makes you feel, etc and the good you're doing, at least then they'll know, it won't stop the worrying but at least they'll know what they're worrying about!"

We knew that he was right and that, maybe, we should tell them, get everything in the open but I did not believe that it was as simple as that. I could see that Terry felt the same way; he had been through this before during his drug baron days and he knew that the least your loved ones knew about what you were doing the safer they would be. It was better if they thought that you were having some illicit night time liaisons rather than the whole truth. It just seemed easier to continue the lie and trust that you do not get found out. We could explain away a bruise or a gash, we got it through some incident playing football, or squash, or badminton or the usual rough house games that alpha males play.

"Sometimes man, you know, it is a lot easier to carry a lie than to explain the trueness of tings to your family. I always ask myself do they need to know? If they don't then it is better you don't tell them. If they is snooping around then if you can't lie safely then and only then tell them some of the truth, you can leave the whole truth to the court room!"

They had convinced me that it would do no good to tell Nicolette what we were doing, also if I told her then I was forcing Terry to tell Eva and then they would tell someone else and so on. I just didn't like lying to her, I must endeavour to have better stories when the need arose and Terry and I needed to ensure we had those stories straight seeing as Nicolette and Eva seemed to be exchanging notes on us.

Jerry changed the topic back to R Kelly asking Terry if he had been to the centre today, Terry said that he hadn't but he had seen some of his cronies. He said that he would watch out for him and to note if there was any change in his behaviour. I silently hoped that he did behave as I didn't fancy going through that again with him, I could still smell him on me, hopefully he will move out of the area and become someone else's problem. Jerry suggested that if we did have to 'regulate' him again that we take extra plastic sheeting and change of clothes.

"And don't forget disinfectant and air freshener!"

"Listen, maybe we could just dash his arse in the River and hold him down for a while, when we finish with him we just let him float downstream?!"

"Or we get him in the centres changing rooms, them showers are pretty good and out of the way of things, he can piss and shit to his hearts content and we'll be clean as well?!"

"Listen, if there is a next time I'm gonna make sure we run his smelly arse out of town!"

I went home with a smile on my face laughing about the many ways that we had come up with to regulate R Kelly, but hoping none of them came to fruition, hoping that he would take on board the message we had tried to deliver to him. I got home, Nicolette was alone in the Lounge watching some documentary with David Attenborough, the kids were already in bed. I took off my shoes and coat, smiled at her; she beckoned my over to her patting the seat on the settee next to her and then held up a glass of wine asking if I wanted some, telling me that the bottle was on the dining table. We drank the wine; snuggled up to each other watching the rest of the documentary.

Things felt good but my mind was working overtime, part of me wanted to tell her there and then what we were doing, the other argued that it was better to keep my counsel. I was sure that she would understand, but then I was not so sure. Finally I decided to keep quiet and make sure that I maintain the stories that there really wasn't any point in her being unduly worried.

Ade Akinfiewia & others chapter 14

*N*ow that I had convinced myself that we had to be a secret and the only moral arguments would be mine with me, I felt more at ease with what it was that we were trying to achieve. I was more content now that we had 'regulated' a few of the miscreants in our midst and wanted to move things on at a quicker pace. Both Terry and Jerry agreed and we set out plans to 'regulate' at least one person a week and to make sure that the message was out in the 'badlands' that they did not have it all their own way anymore, that one day they too may be hauled off the streets and 'regulated'. They would not know when but to be rest assured that it would happen.

We had to make sure that those we had already taken were behaving themselves; I made it my business to check out Johnson Cole to see what he was up to. It wasn't very hard to locate him as he still frequented the usual places. I sat in my car outside the Shooting Star one night waiting for him. It wasn't long before he showed up; he still looked his cocky, drugged up self and still had that fixed scowl on his face. I was beginning to think that we would have to drive him back to the torture chamber.

There was the usual group of men outside the doorway of the pub smoking and laughing and joking, calling out to women walking past, but all generally good natured. Johnson walked up to the group, whereas before he would probably have bounced through them knocking out of his way anyone silly enough not to notice him, this time he stopped and laughed and joked with the group, swapped secret handshakes and touches and then went inside. I could hear a conversation after he went in.

"Him is awright once you get to know him, you know!"

"He quiet down from de idiot a while back, first time me see him smile!"

"Still tek him drugs but him don't seem so drugged up all de time!"

I was surprised, what was said confirmed that we had done the community some good. Here was this out of control drug fiend fighting everyone and anyone who walked on his shadow and now look at him, it worked. Another day I watched him walking down the High Road, whereas he would normally scowl and growl at people he was convinced was weaker than him, this time he kept his head high and walked past, he even smiled at some people as he passed them. I was amazed, not because I did not think that what we were doing was going to work, but that it only took one visit to change Johnson Cole who really was a tough nut.

I met up with Terry and Jerry later in the week and followed up my telephone report to them about Johnson Cole. We high five'd each other and gave each other knowing looks to confirm that what we were doing was the right thing. That, if we could change someone like Johnson Cole then we could force a change in anyone, forgetting the 'Trendy' incident, because we all knew that was a different story altogether.

"Listen the regulators are here to stay man!"

"Certainly makes it all worthwhile, you know what I mean, Dis is why we need to get a move on and do more. We need to quickly identify a few more marks and get on with it!"

"I agree, listen, you two have the inside knowledge about these people you got to start working harder in getting them, then I'll make my tools work harder in sorting them out!"

This experience had given me renewed vigour and convinced me that we had to keep on with our aim. Things were getting worse on the streets, everyday on the news and in the newspapers more incidents of stabbings, beatings, rapes etc. were being reported. More young men being robbed of their lives by the thrust of a blade, or the swing of a fist, or at the bottom of a pack of feral children thirsting for blood. We had to take back our streets make them safe for our families, for our friends, for our neighbours, for everyone. We had to continue to clean up our streets taking the bad lads and giving them tough love.

Over the next few weeks we moved up a gear and were regulating, at least, one person a week. We were very busy and because of this news started to spread through the streets that there was a new gang fighting to take over the streets, who were targeting anyone who considered themselves a 'shotta!' A story had even made the local newspaper, tucked away on page fifteen below an advert extolling the virtues of some well known high street chains locally produced products.

Terry had remarked that we knew we had made it when we are given equal billing to turnips, potatoes and broccoli, but not just any old vegetables, locally produces ones. The article talked about a war on the streets that it needed to be nipped in the bud before it escalated, but it then went on to talk about vigilantism and people should not be taking the law into their own hands. That rather than a street war this was a group of men attacking those they thought to be up to no good. That the reporter had eye witness testimony of a snatch squad in operation and that when the kidnapped are questioned after they would not talk or explain their various injuries. The report ended by stating that the reporter would be passing the information gathered to the police to investigate.

The report talked about a snatch that we had done only the week before, our victim was Ade Akinfiewia, a tall gangly, dark skinned boy only eighteen but had already spent most of the last four years in juvenile detention, mainly for street robberies, holding up girls or young boys for their money, jewellery and mobile phones. His modus was simple, he and his posse would hang around schools or shopping areas looking for likely suspects, kids talking on their phones, or with jewellery or spending money. Anyone could be a victim as long as they were weaker than he and his posse. They would circle their victim like American Indians circling settlers in their wagons.

They would follow their target until they had reached somewhere quiet, usually when they were walking past open space or an alley. Two of them would be walking ahead, keeping in contact with the main group by mobile phone. When their victim was approaching an 'hotspot' they would phone ahead these two would then hold up the victim by engaging them in some sort of dialogue, either asking for a light, or to borrow their phone, if it was girls, pretend to chat them up. Before long the main group would catch up, circle the victim and 'persuade' them to loosen their grip on whatever possessions they had. Ade usually did the talking and he was the ring leader, he took possession of the stolen property and he divided the money amongst the posse.

He had been caught many times because he had become a known face to the local police, so anytime similar robberies occur he would be one of the first hauled in by the police. It was on one of these occasions that he was charged with a robbery and brought to court where I was prosecuting him. I had received the papers that morning picked them up from my desk at the office and rushed to court, having already been warned that it was a full list. I managed to find a quiet space to go through the morning cases and started to read the papers relating to Ade. As I read the papers I could smell a problem, the victims could not or did not want to identify him, all the police had to arrest him was that he had a chain in his pocket that belonged to one of the victims.

His statement said that he had found the chain on a wall only minutes before the police stopped him. He had shown them the wall where they then found in a bush next to the wall the victims purse and mobile phone. He was charged on the strength of being in possession of the chain and being known by the police. I spoke with the police about my fears for the case, they were adamant that it was Ade and his gang because the whole thing fitted their modus and they had arrested him only ten minutes after the robbery so they did not believe his story. I had to tell them that evidentially the case was weak and that if he had a good defence lawyer they would see this as well. I had to tell them that, in my experience if he pleaded not guilty in all likelihood the CPS would drop the charges long before the case came to trial.

They were not very happy but accepted the situation. I think they knew that they would get him again soon, because, as one of them said to me;

"You know these fucking animals they don't know how to do nothing else, we're doing society a favour getting these bastards, the lot 'em, off our streets!"

I read into it what he meant and I instantly disliked him. I knew he wasn't just talking about Ade but he put all non Caucasian types under that umbrella. As far as he was concerned Ade was beef on his table, if he couldn't eat beef today he knew he would have it some time soon and he was licking his lips in anticipation knowing that if it wasn't Ade beef it would be some other 'animal', even me. He looked at me as he said this as if to say 'yeah you and all, do something wrong and I'll take pleasure in cutting you down as well you, your fancy clothes and fancy talk and fancy degree ain't gonna save you…!'

As I had expected Ade's lawyer had noticed the problems in the evidence, I was trying to persuade him to get his client to plead to a reduced and lesser charge with no mention of custody just so that I could get a tick against this case, but they were having none of it. Ade pleaded not guilty as expected, his lawyers parting shot to me was "see you in court, if it ever gets that far!" He knew like I did that this case was going nowhere and Ade was free to carry on robbing. I wasn't actually sure whom I felt sorry for more his next victims or him when that bigoted officer finally caught up with him. It was then that I knew Ade had to be our next target mainly to save him from the retribution of that officer, at least our aim was to regulate him, make him see the error of his ways, give him a lesson in tough love. Whereas the officer just wanted him put away turn him into another statistic another notch on his belt.

Picking him up was easy and once back at the Torture Chamber it was business as usual. Jerry was at his terrifying best. He had found a new tool to use, one that got him up close and personal to Ade. It was the smallest tool on the table but proved the most effective, a pair of pliers, which he used first on Ade's fingers slowly applying pressure with the avowed intent to crush every one of them. He had untied one of his hands shook it firmly in a kind of Masonic handshake then spread the fingers, in the same motion he had clamped the pliers serrated teeth onto his ring finger and started to squeeze applying pressure as he asked him in a quiet but menacing voice to think about all the things he had used this hand for and then think of all those things he would never do again as he was going to make sure that he would not be able to use it again, not even to scratch his balls.

I could feel his pain as Jerry moved from one finger to the other, applying pressure until you could hear the bone cracks. It was at the third finger his little pinky that Ade passed out. Terry had then leaned over him raising his head by placing his hand under his chin and began to slap him with the front of his open hand, striking the left side of his face and in the same flowing motion slapped the right side of his face with the back of his hand. He repeated this motion five or six times until Ade had come around.

At first you could see he did not know where he was, he shook his head and slowly opened his eyes. You could see that he was hoping that this was all some mad nightmare that he was at home in bed and the pain he felt in his hand was because he was laying awkwardly on it. That the bright light shining into his eyes was the streetlight outside his bedroom shining through as he had forgotten, as usual, to pull his curtains before going to sleep. That the angry voice was his father's, scolding him again for some misdemeanour or another, did he leave the lights on, did he forget to lock the back door, or take out the trash.

As Terry slapped him the sixth or seven time it brought him back to reality, it wasn't a dream, we were real and we were really hurting him and asking him to think about his life thus far and if he did not regulate his behaviour we would be back for his next hand and then his toes and then whatever else took our fancy. Jerry then clamped the pliers onto his nose and squeezed hard and asked him again and again if he understood us and asked him what he was going to do about it. He said the right things, said he promised he wouldn't do it again, asked us to leave him alone, implored us to stop, that he wanted to go home, that he didn't want this.

I asked him if he liked being a victim, if he could see how one of his victims felt as he and his posse was stalking them then robbing them. I asked him if he wanted to continue to be a victim, if he did all he had to do was to continue to rob people. He said he understood, his nose now bleeding profusely and Jerry continued to apply pressure, the serrated teeth of the pliers eating into his ample fleshy nose.

When we had finished we loaded him back into the van, me, as usual, in the back and Jerry and Terry in the front the radio pumping out an old time classic and Jerry and Terry singing along. "Ain't no stopping us now...." When the van came to a stop and Jerry opened the back I was surprised to see that we were at the hospital. Jerry pulled Ade out of the van by his legs, untied the sack and softly told him that we were at the hospital and he should go and get his hand checked out, but just to emphasise that we were still in control of him Jerry slapped him hard around the back of his head and pushed him in the general direction of the Accident and Emergency department. I then squeezed into the front of the van with them.

We went to our usual place to unwind and talk about the past events. We were all on our usual high and laughed and joked about Ade. Jerry called him a tough son of a bitch as many others would have cracked completely after what we did to him. I asked Terry how come we stopped at the hospital, we didn't normally feel that sorry for our targets.

"It wasn't me man, it was Jerry, kept going on about his hand and how he should have it looked at. Dat if we left him he was such a tough guy he wouldn't go to the hospital so kept on at me until I stopped there."

"Listen, don't get me wrong I don't feel sorry for him he got what was coming to him, but I definitely broke three of his fingers and he needed them setting and stuff. I heard what you said about him, that it was tough love we was giving him, so I gave him a chance. Believe this though, if he fucks up I will take his other fingers and his bastard toes next time, so don't go thinking that I've gone soft!"

I agreed with him, I had told them about the police man and what he had said in court. I had told them that if we did not do something for this kid he would never be turned around and would then be at the mercy of people like that policeman for the rest of his life. I had told them that we were actually going to save a life tonight, he may not appreciate it now but in time to come he will realise that we did him a massive favour.

I fully believe and still do that we had saved Ade from other horrors if he had continued down that path, yes we were doing this to make the streets safer and to get the rotten apples out of the barrel, but equally we were doing this for the kids like Ade, saving them from themselves. Terry had said that it was like their continued criminality was really a cry for help and we were only too willing to answer that cry for help and turn them around using the only language that they could understand – violence.

We were a little surprised to see that he had spoken with a journalist, but we felt elated that our work had been publicised. The fact that Ade had spoken to a journalist meant to us that he had taken heed of our message, that this was a sign that he was turning his back on crime.

A few days later we were in our usual place planning our next move, Terry had said that he had some news for us regarding Ade and the article in the local newspaper. Apparently, this journalist spent most of his time hanging around the hospitals A & E department sniffing out a good story. He was there when Ade walked in, after we had dropped him off, because his injuries were not serious he had to sit around in the waiting area for hours, which was typical for that hospital many a time I had been there to get checked over for a sprained ankle or damaged finger, but left frustrated without being seen because the wait is so long.

The journalist noticed him and persuaded him to talk about what had happened to him, hoping that he would get some gory tale of a street fight or some drug feud he was instead regaled by Ade about being tortured by a gang, taken to some sort of torture chamber looking like something out of a gothic tale. That there were three men, he believed at least two of them were Black because of their accents, one he was not sure about, but that he did not know who they were.

The journalist had pressed him time and again to talk about what had happened and tried to make him admit that this was some gangland feud, which he had been caught up in and he was just making all this torture chamber stuff up, as he thought it was pie in the sky fanciful that anyone would have this sort of thing in the 21st century. Ade had told him that he was not in any gang but that we were some new faces on the street clearing the patch for ourselves and that he was an innocent victim. He was so adamant that the journalist half believed his story and pressed him for more details.

He had told the journalist that he was now scared and even if he was into crime before he now would not be as we had scared him sufficiently to keep his nose clean. The journalist was not sure whether to believe Ade which is why he wrote the article the way he did. Was it a new gang on the streets or was it really a vigilante group attempting to clean up the neighbourhood?

"This guy actually came to my centre to interview me asking me if I had heard about a vigilante group in the neighbourhood, telling me about his encounter with Ade to try and get me to confirm it one way or the other he even described the torture chamber. Of course, I told him that I hadn't heard anything, but he was very persistent saying he had to get to the bottom of this."

"Listen, this is crap man, no way are they gonna locate us, you got the story of one scared kid, who some journo half believes. Even if they had ten of our targets how they gonna find us?"

"Hey man, I ain't worried man, don't fret, is nothing. You is right can't no-one put us in it, the only one who knows about us is Weekes and he is hardly gonna speak with some journo or de man dem, is he?"

I sat and listened as Jerry and Terry bantered about being in the papers and the effect it would have on some of the villains in the area knowing that someone was out to get them. Unlike them, I was scared not at being found out, but that because certain villains may start thinking we could go after them that we would have to resort to even more violence just to get them into the van, let alone what we would have to do once we got them back to the torture chamber. I must admit that the idea of a journalist on our trail was quite intriguing and it brought a smile to my face as I imagined him snooping around the streets and drug dens asking the questions no other journalist would dare ask in his search for a scoop that would take him out of the backwoods of local journalism and to his rightful place working for the Mirror, the Sun or even the Daily Star!

Nevertheless we had to be careful, although I agreed with Terry that the majority of our targets would not be as loose at the mouth as Ade and would probably have threatened the journalist with violence if he had persisted with asking them questions. I couldn't see Robert Kelly answering questions'

"Excuse me sir how did you come by those injuries…. And what? What is that smell, phew? What made you shit yourself sir?"

"Well you see I got dragged off the streets and beaten to a pulp by these three guys, who scared me so much I shat myself... Hey where you going where's my money for my story, I've got more to tell you...!"

"Listen, that's funny man. You know maybe we should respond anonymously to the article, you know get that journo's taste buds going, give him something that will make him write some more. We could give him some names, use him to do part of our job of keeping an eye on some of them guys kind of like a surreptitious message to them that we are still out there watching them, what do you think?"

I was dead against the idea; the more anonymous we remained the better it was. By us responding to the story would have been a direct admission that we were out there. He only had one tiny piece of a story from one person who could quite easily have been embellishing what had happened to them, by writing to him and giving names meant that we were going public and it would make our job harder because we would then be the hunted, we would have to be looking over our shoulders every time we decided to go out regulating.

Terry agreed with me and said to Jerry that he must be mad and had he thought about what it would be like if we were found out, we would have to leave the area or even the country, the amount of people who would want to get even with us. Not forgetting that what we had done so far was simply grievous bodily harm, let alone getting implicated in the death of 'Trendy'. Eventually Jerry agreed with us, but not until we reminded him that the more we went public we would have less opportunity to regulate anyone and he would spend less time in the torture chamber with his beloved tools.

*O*ver the next couple of weeks further stories appeared in the local paper all hinting at a possible vigilante gang, but nothing concrete was reported on and we carried on regardless. The journalist had been to see Terry a few more times, but he seemed more interested in the project and the work Terry did. His questions to Terry were more to do with youth crime and the latest wave of stabbings. It seemed to Terry that he had latched onto Terry to use him as a vehicle to get onto one of the bigger newspapers, that if he had Terry's confidence as and when, and in his mind it was only a matter of when, a youth got stabbed in the area he could get the full "low down" direct from Terry. Then he could sell his story to a red top and then he would be off out of the local circuit.

We regulated one a week some times two. The roll of honour read like an who's who of villains in the area; Lee Jenson, Livingstone Kenworth, Morgan Mugabe, Benjamin Sithole, Ife Manu, Blair Brown, Yohannes Qatada, and others with more fancy names, the double barrelled, the street monickers. I remembered their names, I remembered their crimes, I kept a ledger locked away in my desk at home. It was becoming easier and became something of a routine for us; we had certainly perfected the routine. My only nagging feeling was that Jerry had become too used to the violence and had increased the intensity after each victim. Terry and I had resolved to back each other in case we had to jump in if we felt that he was going too far.

He seemed to have a penchant for fingers and toes and repeated the punishment he had meted out to Ade on at least another four occasions, especially on the street robbers who he had very little sympathy for and if they did not scream he was not happy. He then seemed to get bored crunching digits replacing this with smashing their toes with a large mallet the type that would not go amiss on a fairground stall. When he first did this I recoiled in horror and can still hear the screams of pain from his victim. He painted a sorry sight for weeks to come plastered up just below his knee. But, we were memorable and the punishment meted out to them would not be forgotten in a hurry, nor the lesson we force fed them, if they wanted to re-offend then they knew what to expect, but they did not know when it would happen or who was inflicting it on them.

The problem was that I could not berate Jerry for 'going too far' because this whole situation was unreal, we were using violence to cure the recalcitrant and recidivist amongst us, as they were using violence to scare and terrorise our neighbourhood. If what Jerry was doing was working in enforcing our message to these street rogues then how could I tell him to ease up and not be so brutal? Experience had hardened me to accept that in order to be my brothers' keeper I must incur on them great vengeance and furious anger, Jerry was certainly enlivening this. How else were we to enforce our message, if it wasn't meeting their violence with our own, which had to be more forceful, more nefarious than what they could ever inflict on anyone else.

We seemed to be having an impact on the area as there was another report in the local paper, which had a picture of the leader of the council the Chief Superintendent for the area and the Mayor crowing about how the council had set up joint initiatives with the police which had meant a dramatic drop in reported crime in the area. They slapped each other on the backs at how they had come up with the ideas and both were insistent on pursuing them despite local community organisations claiming that they were ill thought out and could make things worse.

The leader of the council was reported as saying;

"…but we remained strong to our beliefs and pushed through the initiatives, the results of which you can all see now, our streets are the safest in London. You can depend on us, you can depend on the local police force, we have your interests at heart and we will not stop until everyone feels safe on our streets not just during the day but through the night as well. This is our signal to anyone with ill intent in their mind, don't do it we are watching you and we are coming to get you!!"

Terry, Jerry and I had a good laugh about that and asked what the crime figures would have been had we not been so active with our own brand of crime fighting, would their initiative have meant a damned thing if we were not persuading the villains to go straight. The difficult thing about all of this was that we all wanted to shout out what we were doing and be part of the self congratulating party being thrown, but we knew, as well, that we had to remain quiet in order that our good work could continue.

It would be so easy to declare publicly what we were doing, hold a press conference, provide the evidence then ask for the public and local politics to back us in our work. However, we knew that it would not be like that; we and our families would be in immediate danger, not forgetting that what we were doing was illegal and could get us a long prison sentence. So silent we remained, silently taking the plaudits, silently slapping each other on the back, silently popping the champagne corks, and holding our own self congratulatory party, writing our own headlines and waving back at the cheering throng of people hailing us as saviours, we are our brothers' keepers.

Nelson, Tyrone and Alton chapter 15

It had been a crazy few weeks; I was feeling tired and was running out of excuses to my wife. I had spoken with Terry and he admitted to feeling the pace as well. Nicolette and Eva were meeting up and talking more and we knew that this meant that they were suspicious of us. We had met up at our local, Jerry was late as usual. I knew I had to raise the issue of having a quiet spell, but wasn't sure how Jerry would take it, as he had really been into the last few weeks. Terry supported me so Jerry had to reluctantly agree to a ceasefire of sorts. I told him that we had regulated so many in the last few weeks that we hadn't had time to stand back to see the effect of our 'campaign'. I told him that we needed to now keep an eye out to ensure they hadn't gone back to old ways, otherwise it would have been a glorious waste of time and we would be no better than them.

"I agree with Barry, Jerry, we need to see if t'ings is holding and not splitting at the seams. We've been so busy I t'ink we need to see what we is doing and mek sure dat it is working. Do we have to re-visit anyone and besides the missus is thinking we is up to all sorts!"

"Listen, I can understand what you guys is saying, but we're too far into this to stand back now. But, yeah, okay I think we need to look at some of dese boys again and make sure they're doing the right thing. Listen, I can think of a few I would like to get my hands on again!"

He stood up as he was saying this and nodded in agreement, but he added that it should not be longer than two weeks otherwise they would think that we have stopped and that they can get up to their nonsense again. He added that if there was anyone who had not taken on board our message then we should not waste time but get them straight away. His passing shot at both Terry and I was;

"Listen, you guys should manage your women better!"

Then he was off, we both nodded to him and smiled, I know what Terry was thinking. I wanted to call him back and explain what commitment meant, but I knew he wouldn't listen. However, he brought back to mind how I had been lying to Nicolette all this time, but I knew I had to continue to lie to her for all our sakes. It did feel sort of sordid, like I was having an affair of sorts, but not the conventional type of affair. I wasn't shagging the typist or clerk at the office in the broom cupboard and I wasn't sitting in some wine bar hidden away with my new love interest, sipping red wine and surreptitious planning my getaway to a new life with my new woman. I was actually surreptitiously planning a better life for my wife and family, clearing the fear of violence from the streets so that it was safer for them, my noble crusade.

Our overalls were our own version of shiny silver suits of armour, the van our trusted steed, the tools in the chamber our weapons of choice to mete out justice in the name of every decent, law abiding family, who wanted to live their lives free to walk the streets without fear, have a laugh without the threat of violence, theft or robbery. Ezekiel 25:17 became known to us as our charter, the vigilantes charter, wherever and whenever our victims heard this they would remember us. They will get a cold chill down their spine and flash furtive glances over their shoulders and at every junction. They knew that we were watching them, monitoring their progress because we told them we would not just let them walk the streets free from any retribution if they continued to sin.

I had every intention to adhere to our agreement and take a break, let the grass grow in order that we could monitor our previous targets. We met regularly to swap notes on our previous targets; Robert Kelly had gone back to college and was studying to become an electrician. He and his crew had approached Terry asking if he would help them set up a recording studio as they wanted to pursue their music. As Robert wasn't very talented musically but was reasonably good with his hands and on computers they had elected him as their sound man, which meant he had to go back to college to obtain the necessary knowledge to carry out the function properly.

Terry had described his meeting with them and how they were all adamant that they had turned away from crime and wanted to do something that would improve their lot. Terry had asked them what had changed their minds, but they went coy at this, but all looked at Robert as if to say, 'ask him, we don't want what happened to him to happen to us'.

That had brought a smile to Terry's face and he nodded knowingly to show that he understood them. He agreed to let them use one of the unused offices in the centre, but they had to do all the work to sound proof it and turn it into a recording studio. He would help them secure some funding for the equipment, but he reminded them that he would not tolerate any knocked off stuff or any wrong doing.

"The first stink of stupidness and you is gone, if we do dis we do it neat, you get me?!"

"Nah man we don't do dem tings, we is serious 'bout getting dis ting going, it's gonna be good for our 'ends man, we is aiming for MTV Base keep watching we'll be there!"

Some of the others had gone completely to ground; we had gone to their usual haunts but couldn't find them anywhere. We had heard through the grapevine that Livingstone and Brown had packed their bags and moved North in the case of Brown and to the Caribbean in the case of Livingstone. Maybe there they can carry on being the bad boys they thought they were and out of our clutches. Mugabe we heard had been shipped back to Africa by his concerned parents.

They had found him the morning after hardly able to walk after having some of his toes crushed by us. His Father who was a preacher at the local branch of the Church of Jesus the Lion had been concerned for a while about his son's activities had found him on coming back from a prayer meeting; a special prayer meeting which he had set up to pray for his son's salvation and deliverance (seems like his prayer was answered 'mysteriously'). On seeing his son in such a state he rushed him to hospital and whilst he was being treated had purchased a one way ticket to Zambia arranging for his care with his grandmother and with the church. Mugabe had no say in the move and even if he did, I doubt that, after his 'regulation' he would have wanted to stay.

We had certainly had an affect on him, after slapping and beating him and threatening to burn his face Jerry then got to work on his toes. He couldn't see what was happening to his toes; he just felt it as Jerry systematically crushed each chosen digit. After four toes he would have agreed to anything, screaming in pain he even denounced Satan and expressed his love of Jesus. He kept calling us brother, it was then that I realised he thought we were members of his father's church hired to bring him back into the fold.

His father had threatened him many times that he would do anything to bring him back, 'back to life' he would call it and he thought that this was the finale of his father's sojourn. That if he did not repent then he would not see another day break as these men will surely kill him, in the name of the Lord. So when the first person he saw after his regulation was his father he knew it was true and realised, in his own mind, how much this man loved him. He went willingly to Zambia.

Lee Jenson was as tough as old boots, I remembered his regulation was the toughest one we had, it took all three of us to get him into and out of the van. We hit him with everything and apart from sweating profusely he never cried out he simply stared at us as if to say "is that all you got...?" I remember Jerry getting very frustrated, he kept going back to the tool table and coming back with even more weaponry to test on Lee Jenson, but he remained stoic throughout. This was until, out of nowhere Terry drew a gun, I say out of nowhere because that is how it seemed one minute I was beating a tattoo on his chest and midriff, Jerry was behind him throttling him with some sort of nylon wire, then the next a gun had been shoved into his mouth. The silence was deafening as we heard the click of the pistol being loaded, the catch being pulled back.

"Now I fucking have your attention, you Mudder musta beat you like a junkyard dawg every fucking day, but bet she nebber did nuttin' like dis. You raas you is ready to listen fe we, nod you fucking head or I will blow your fucking head clean off now!"

I found myself nodding as Terry continued in a loud but steady voice, the muzzle of the pistol still in Lee Jenson's mouth, letting him know who we were, why we were doing this to him, what we will do to him if he doesn't amend his ways and finally;

"You t'ink I wont do it, den test me, not one raas bloodclaat man gawn hear you scream, not one bloodclaat man gon find you body if you choose not fe listen to we, now you know!"

He nodded his head, looking cross eyed at the pistol shoved firmly into his mouth he looked into Terry's eyes but could not find any solace, anything to hold onto, at that moment; as far as he was concerned he was a dead man. He almost cried when Terry pulled the gun from his mouth and shouted at Jerry and I to let him go. He couldn't talk but his face said it all, told us that he promised to behave himself, that he wasn't going to burgle old people's homes and take pleasure in beating them up, or threaten young children until they stole for him. He made a thousand promises to get out of the gang culture, turn in his colours, even to go to church.

After we had dropped off Lee Jenson I couldn't hold it in any longer I had to ask Terry where the gun had come from and why he was packing it.

He told us that he had found it in the van after we had regulated Livingstone Kenworth, he didn't tell us because he felt that we didn't need to know, but as we were regulating more and more dangerous villains he felt it may come in useful one day as protection for all us.

"Come on guys, this is our protector, what you gonna do if some one opens up on us. It could happen, look at some of de shits we have been pulling up lately. And look at dat guy he weren't afraid until I shove the piece in his mouth. We need dis piece."

I reluctantly agreed, but got him to promise that he wouldn't use it unless we all agreed. We were suppose to be regulating these guys not killing them, in my mind that was the final sanction and we should leave that for others with less morals than us. Jerry was quite taken aback and begged to see it, Terry gave it to him to hold. I then added another proviso that Jerry doesn't get his hands on it whilst we were regulating he had looked like he wanted to use it too much. Lee Jenson was as good as his word, from our vantage point in the shadows he looked to have turned over a new leaf. He was still hanging around the estate, smoked his spliff and looked every bit the bad guy, but now he walked away when his friends talked about chivving someone or turning over someone's drum. All he needed now was a chance at a job and his metamorphosis would be complete.

It wasn't until we had agreed to take the break that I realised that I needed it. I had to think of a new excuse, I had told Nicolette that I had started playing football with Terry's youth club team, which allowed us two nights a week for training. As I wasn't very good I had become more of the coach and trainer, then on the weekends I would be the substitute only needed if we didn't have enough players or someone got injured. Terry was always the more natural athlete and was the best striker in the district. Now, as he got older, he was probably the best centre half in the area. Luckily for us the 'break' coincided with the end of season so I did not have to make any excuses why I would be home more in the evenings. She had seemed happy enough and made the usual jokes about my hairy and knobbly knees, even offering me massages after games. She had even come down to a couple of games to cheers us on, but got bored of all the macho posturing, that she thought went with football, she couldn't understand how men got so worked up about a little game.

*J*erry called every other day to ask if I had finished my rest and whether I was ready to get back out there, telling me that there were more villains out there waiting for us and how our journalist friend had gone quiet. I could tell from his voice that he was itching to get back to the Torture Chamber, but he respected our wish and knew that he couldn't simply force us out. However, things began to take a more different route than I had expected. I expected to lay and rest for a month or so, watch a few of our victims and give myself time to draw up a new list of potential victims and time to then watch them and plan how we would get them off the streets. The fact that the journalist seemed to have got bored and gone onto pastures new was a good thing and made me more content that the rest was a good idea.

Unknown to Jerry and I, Terry had been meeting with Alton Weekes who had been keeping a watch over us and our activities. He had become interested in what we were doing, especially as we seemed to have cleared away some problems for him. It seems that Benjamin Sithole and Yohannes Qatada had been upsetting him because they were able to get hold of cheaper forms of drugs and were underselling him. This we did not know as we had regulated both of them because they had got away with a violent assault on two boys (Tunde Longe and Kyle Ritchie) who attended Terry's community centre and with whom he had turned around from crime and had used them as examples of how a positive image can work for disadvantaged kids. They had got into an argument with Sithole and Qatada about them pestering youngsters at the community centre to buy drugs from them. They had 'urged' these two to do their selling elsewhere and not at the centre. As they were bigger than Sithole and Qatada they easily forced them away from the centre and everyday would 'face off' with them so that they couldn't sell their illegal wares.

Terry had warned them to watch their backs as these guys would not take them pushing them out of their patch sitting down. They were both confident that nothing would happen to them as the other kids would be their eyes and ears. Unfortunately, this was not enough as a few nights later they were driving in Tunde's car, music blaring loud when they were rear ended by a large 4 x 4 and pushed off the road straight into a lamppost.

As neither was wearing seatbelts they both hit the windscreen with force causing them head injuries. Both were near unconsciousness when their attackers leapt from their 4 x 4, one started to slash at Tunde with a large blade the other began hitting Kyle with what looked like a wheel brace. They only managed to get off a couple of hits as people began milling around and shouting that the police had been called, before jumping back into their 4 x 4 and driving off with tyres screeching. As they ran off they were heard to shout out;

"You t'ink you is bad now, keep your bill out of our business!"

Both were hospitalised and Terry visited them everyday, warning them about seeking retribution, telling them the police would handle it, they knew who it was and there are witnesses, encouraging them to use all their efforts to get well quickly. Unfortunately, no one came forward who could positively identify either Sithole or Qatada and they were eventually charged with dangerous driving and causing an accident. In court they pleaded guilty to these charges and received a suspended sentence and 200 hours community service. Terry went apoplectic with rage and demanded that we do something about it and it had to be both of them together. I was a little reluctant because of the logistics we had never done two together before, what if one of them got away.

Terry told us not to worry as he had a plan that was sure to work and that they would both come quietly. It seemed that they did most of their deals from their car and as they had got rid of the only opposition in the area they acted like untouchables. They were always parked on a side road adjacent to the Centre, away from houses and out of view of the main road. When they were not selling they would be sitting in the car listening to music and often nodding off, so secure did they feel.

The plan was that Jerry and I will wait in the van at the top of the road and Terry would watch from a vantage point in the gardens of the Centre, it was usual for them to nod off to sleep around 7pm when business was at its slackest. He would then drive the van and park it right next to them, at this point Jerry and I would jump out and grab them both simultaneously and then into the van.

It worked perfectly within seconds they were both hooded up and into the van and we were on our way to the Torture Chamber. We sat them opposite each other so that they could see each others pain. We mainly left Terry to it as they had hurt his boys, he even frightened me with the level of violence he meted out, and how silent he was as he did it. It was left to Jerry and I to explain to them their 'crimes' and who we were I spoke directly to Sithole and jerry took Qatada. As we spoke Terry kept on beating them even pushing us out the way to get to them.

We had to stop him and managed to persuade him to wait in the van, that he had done enough. We then told them that if they didn't listen to us we would leave them alone with Terry if they wanted that all they had to do was to tell us to shut up, they listened and nodded in agreement as we 'encouraged' them not to stray from the righteous path. Selling drugs and beating up good citizens just wasn't on. At this Terry came back in, still in a rage, Jerry and I blocked his way and struggled to keep him from attacking them again.

"You bloodclaat raases if I see any ah you in dis neighbourhood I gahn kill you, you get me you is dead, let me kill dem now, come on…!"

It looked like they had got the message as they hadn't been seen for a while, which is why Terry was speaking with Alton Weekes whom was impressed with what we were doing and wanted us to help him with a 'little problem' that he would deal with himself but he was being watched by various police units. Terry had at first tried to resist him and tell him that we only regulated those who needed persuading to amend their ways, that we were not for hire at any price.

He had told him that we were not mercenaries and could he not hire some hired gun from outside the area to do his work. Alton had told him that he had thought about this but he knew somehow someway it would get back to him, but that we were perfect for this as no-one, apart from him, knew who we were or that we actually existed. He left promising that he would persuade Terry to do this thing for him.

He visited Terry three more times each occasion more demanding than the next, until the last meeting when he informed Terry that we could not use the Torture Chamber anymore. Straightaway Terry knew what this meant, but to acquiesce to Alton's demands would mean that we would be in his pocket that if we could do one we could do more for him. Terry knew he had to let us know what had been going on. We met up at the usual place; as usual we had to wait for Jerry. Whilst waiting Terry was very quiet he just about said hallo to me so I left him to his thoughts and read my newspaper until Jerry arrived.

"Listen, what's happened you guys look like you've had a lover's tiff, what is with all the mystery Terry?"

Terry didn't know how to tell us so just decided to let it all out as it happened. He told us how Alton had thanked us for getting rid of Sithole and Qatada for him, that it was something he was working on but we had beaten him to it and how he praised us for not killing them as he surely would have done. Then he explained how they had had two further meetings and Alton wanting us to solve a problem that he had, how he had refused him out of hand, explaining to him what our mission was and that neither Barry nor Jerry would agree to this. Then he told us that if we didn't agree to it we would not be able to use the Torture Chamber and that he seemed to make the threat that he would make us public knowledge.

Jerry flew into a rage; the thought of never being able to use the Torture Chamber again was too much for him. He demanded that Terry set up a meeting with him so that he could speak with him and he more or less said that he would agree to do anything if it meant us holding onto the Torture Chamber. I was very reluctant to lose the Chamber, but I could not accept the fact that we were being blackmailed by Alton. I asked Terry what he thought would happen if we did this little thing for him, as I knew it meant we would be doing more and more little things for him and then God knows what we would end up in. If by saying no we lost the Chamber then so be it, we would find somewhere else.

Both Jerry and Terry disagreed with me; they couldn't see where we could find somewhere else like the Chamber, which was simply perfect for what we were doing. They felt that the only alternative to saying no was that our Star Chamber would have to be disbanded and neither of them was ready for that just yet. I tried to argue against them but they remained solid. I asked them what about the next time and the time after that, how are we going to ensure that he would not approach us again and again. Terry's idea was to get something on him, it was clear that he was being watched by the police if we could get something of value to the person we were going to help him with and keep this safe maybe we could use that against him. The problem with this idea was that we did not know what or who it was that Alton wanted us to sort out for him so to get something to link to Alton was going to be difficult, but meant we had to agree to the job then in the middle of it we would then have to find that precious something to hold against him. Reluctantly I had to agree to go ahead and be Alton's problem solver and go ahead with the master plan on the proviso that we have a plan B, which involved looking around for a new Torture Chamber so that we would not be held to ransom again by the likes of Alton Weekes, or anyone else who might stumble on our secret.

Alton would not meet with Jerry and I, as far as he was concerned Terry was his man and he saw no reason to speak with Jerry and I, whom he had no affinity with. He was happy when Terry informed him that we agreed to help him and remained happy when Terry told him very firmly that this was a once only deal and once done our debt to him for letting us use the Torture Chamber was fully paid up now and in the future. He agreed to it all and said very quietly that our secret was safe with him.

He then let Terry know what he wanted us for, he had found out who had killed his little brother, the police knew who he was but couldn't do anything because there were no witnesses just the street mathematicians putting two and two together and this guy's name kept cropping up. Immediately after his brother's murder this guy had fled the country, but he was back now giving him the chance to avenge his brother's murder. He would not give Terry his name or any details about him until he was satisfied that it was time to get him, until then we had to wait for him to give us the nod. Terry had pressed him for more information about the murderer, but Alton would only say;

"You guys are into correcting the wrongs in the community, my brother's death was a wrong and you need to sort it out like you've been doing with all the others, you can't judge my brother as he has already been judged, you guys have got to do this thing for me if you really believe what it is that you stand for, I can't do it cos I'm being watched if anyone sees me with him that's it game over for me and for you!"

I remained unhappy at this set-up, first we agreed a break so that we could get our focus back, we had scouted previous victims and all seemed to be going well. Now Alton Weekes has become involved and using us to do his dirty work. I told Jerry that I was concerned that we were moving from vigilante to mercenary and it didn't feel right, worse still the person we are doing the job for is acting all like Charlie from Charlie's angels and only talking to his Bosley, we were out of the loop and expected to perform like seals at a fairground show. Jerry felt the same way, he wasn't happy that we were not in control of our destiny that we were being dictated to by Alton Weekes.

"Listen, I can't say that his little brother deserved to die, but he pissed off a lot of people running around doing whatever he wanted just because of who he was. He was a little shit who thought that he was untouchable, but someone proved that he wasn't. But, I feel Weekes' pain if someone harmed Nelson I would not be in control if I caught up with them, yeah so I understand him. Listen, What I don't understand is why he ain't doing this himself, never mind that he might get caught by the Police I would have thought that vengeance for his brother would outweigh that."

It was another week before Terry gave us further news from Alton. Apparently Alton wasn't ready for us just yet; he wanted this guy to know that he knew who he was and what he did. He wanted to scare him, in fact, he wanted to do more than that, he wanted to get into his psyche, let him know that he was going to suffer just like how his brother had suffered, but he would not know when. One day when he was chilling with his friends, walking down the road, shopping with his mum or even about to get romantic with his girlfriend, Weekes will be there taking his revenge. He wanted him to know what it felt like to be pursued before feeling cold hard steel.

As we were on a hiatus Jerry had taken the opportunity to try to bond more with Nelson. He started taking him out to various gigs or for a father and son drink; he had even tried to get him on a double date with a younger sister of one of his girls. Nelson was not keen on that telling his father that he has a girlfriend and that after what she had been going through he would not be cheating on her. Jerry tried to persuade him that it wasn't cheating it was simply a night out with his father and two women were going to keep them company.

He tried asking him what he meant by what his girlfriend had gone through but Nelson would only say that it was private and that he wouldn't understand. Jerry kept on at him and he finally relented on one condition that he could bring a friend along, just in case he didn't like the company. Jerry agreed, keen to actually be going out with his son and if it didn't go well at least he had the women as a distraction, he wasn't sure about another person, but thought it might make the evening interesting.

Jerry was introduced to Tyrone Salisha's brother, he had to ask who Salisha was. Nelson looked at him with a stare that simply said "typical" and explained to him again that Salisha was his girlfriend, she had gone away for a while but now she is back. Jerry nodded and said;

"Uh, her, I remember, listen, I told you she'd come back to you no girl can stay away from an Asamoah, once we've been there we can always get back in, it must be our pure African genes that do it don't you think boy?"

Nelson wasn't impressed and gave his Father another withering look as if to say "I am nothing like you and never will be!" Jerry ignored it and shook Tyrone's hand and leading him still holding his hand to meet the ladies, who were waiting for them in the bar. He introduced Tyrone first as his 'new son' just found him today and Nelson as his 'first and best son' then went to get in the drinks. Nelson sat quietly in the corner seat leaving a space between himself and the women, ostensibly for his father to sit, but really he wanted to keep enough space between himself and temptation as the younger of the women was very pretty and well dressed. He thought to himself that on another day he might even have tried to 'chirps' her, but not today, not now whilst Salisha was still in so much pain.

Noting his indifference the girl started to give all her attention to Tyrone who was lapping it up, in no time they were deep in conversation. Much to the chagrin of Nelson who sat between his father on his left hand laughing and joking with this woman he had never met, but knew where she would be spending the night and Tyrone canoodling with this PYT on his right, where rightly he should be but for Tyrone's sister. He had fleeting conversations with his father but he was more interested in the women and try as he might he could not even attract Tyrone's attention, he felt like a gooseberry, but he knew that it was his fault, maybe he should not have bought Tyrone along.

Eventually Tyrone prised himself away from the girl and made his way to the toilet, Nelson watched him as he made his way through to the back of the Bar where the toilets were situated. He felt the younger women eyeing him and turned and smiled at her and told her that Tyrone had been a little troubled recently and that it was nice to hear him laugh and see him enjoying himself. Five minutes had passed and Tyrone still wasn't back, Nelson kept watching out for his silhouette to appear weaving its way through the crowd but still no sign of him. Another three minutes and still no Tyrone, Nelson was really worried, but the young lady simply smiled and told him that Tyrone was probably only having a zipper malfunction and that maybe he should go and help him. Nelson was about to rise when he saw Tyrone running from the toilets shoving people out of the way and causing a commotion as he hurried towards them.

Tyrone's hair and face were dripping wet, his clothes were dishevelled as if he had been sleeping in them all night, he was white as a sheet and mumbled something about an accident, grabbed his jacket and ran out of the bar. Nelson apologised to the women and told his father that he had better go to him and get him home, he said goodbye and dashed out after Tyrone. He finally caught up with him and asked him what had happened, he had to ask him a few times before Tyrone said in a voice so quiet he had to get very close to him to hear him.

"Weekes knows it was us, he knows it was us, he knows, he's on to us, can't hide no more, have to face up, fuck that's it, this is it!"

It finally began to dawn on Nelson what he meant, who he meant; a cold shudder went through his body. All he wanted to do was get home, get to the sanctuary of home; surely he would be safe there. He looked behind him, he looked left then right, it didn't look like they were being followed. He told Tyrone to get home and they would meet up the next day. He ran home as fast as he could and slammed the door shut snapping on the safety latch, into his bedroom and immediately under the covers. Dark thoughts hovered above his head full of blood and gore; he could see the face of Junior Shotta as he shoved the blade hard into his stomach.

He remembered how he felt that it went in so easily, something in his mind had said to him "wow that was just like a knife through butter!" Pulling it out he found it harder and noisier a loud squelching noise emanated as he pulled the knife out, then the screaming, a loud piercing scream that brought him to his senses, made him look at what he had done. Tyrone had looked at him as well and they both turned and ran, still holding the knives.

He still had them, hidden underneath his wardrobe his macabre souvenirs of a night he would never forget. Now his life was in danger and he never felt as alone as he did right now. He thought about asking his father, Jerry for help, but thought what could he do against these gangsters. He thought about running, but where to, he couldn't survive in Africa he knew he was too English for that. He resolved he would simply wait for the eleventh hour and pit his wits and hopefully he will survive.

Whilst he was going through this Tyrone was at home, he had reached his front door and quickly entered the house there he sat in the hallway back against the door sobbing quietly to himself. The message from Alton Weekes running over and over again through his mind.

"I know you, I know who you are, you took a life, a life that meant something to me, and I'm gonna tek yours, not now, but soon. You got nowhere to run, nowhere to hide cos I'm gonna get you sucka!"

As his head was being continuously flushed into the toilet by one of Alton Weekes bodyguards. Each time this happened Weekes was kicking him hard on his kidneys and then when they had finished and he had slumped to the floor of the toilet cubicle Weekes had stamped on his head then grabbed him by the nape of his neck and issued what Tyrone saw as his epitaph;

"You think revenge is sweet well my revenge is sweeter!"

They then let him out and laughed as he struggled to his feet, slipping and sliding on the wet floor. It took him three attempts to stand straight another few seconds to steady himself then he was off like a hare out of the traps. Nothing was going to stop him until he reached the safety of home his sanctuary. He wouldn't have stopped for Nelson but he was so out of breathe and his side had started to hurt, it felt like stitch but he knew it was from where Weekes had been kicking him.

His head was pounding and continued to pound even after he had reached the sanctuary of home. He had stopped sobbing he knew he couldn't now run away again they must be watching him, it was now just a matter of time. He resolved to wait to 'man up' and hopefully he will survive.

He remembered the night as clearly as if it had happened just this morning. They had cornered him and started beating him, berating him for what he done to Salisha. Somehow he had got free of them and started running they chased him. Nelson being so fit had caught up to him first. By the time he had caught up Nelson had already stabbed him, one blow to his midriff. He was surprised that there wasn't much blood at first then he noticed the first red stain on Junior Shotta's clothes, something clicked in his brain and as Junior Shotta slumped forward he slashed at him catching him with the point of the knife across his chest, cutting deep through his clothes, he could feel the rending of flesh as the knife ran its course across Junior Shotta's chest. By now he was bleeding profusely, Nelson had already started running, he turned and chased after him.

They vowed not to mention this night to anyone and told Nelson that he and Salisha will be gone by the morning, that no-one knew him or would think he was involved so he had to stay and be strong. Nelson wanted to know how long they would be gone, he didn't know but told him one month, hoping that by then everything would have calmed down. Something inside him said never to return, but he knew what he had done and he knew, even then that he would have to face up to it one day, that day, he thought, was rapidly approaching.

Jerry had phoned Nelson the next morning to find out what had happened and why they had run out, Nelson mentioned something about Tyrone getting a call from his sister saying that his mother was sick; he was worried as she hadn't been well for a while. By the time he had caught up with him and he had explained what had happened he couldn't be bothered to return to the bar. He had mumbled an apology to Jerry and hoped he hadn't ruined his evening, but seeing that he hadn't tried to call him last night he knew that he hadn't. He thought how typical, I could have been in all sorts of trouble but his first thoughts' was to getting laid, what a father.

*T*erry had continued to meet with Alton Weekes and was feeding back to Jerry and I any information he thought was relevant. Jerry was beginning to get suspicious of Terry, that he was getting too friendly with Alton and forgetting about us. I had to remind him that Terry had to keep him 'sweet' and if he didn't we would not have the use of the Torture Chamber' and that Alton may spill the beans about what we have been doing. I told him not to judge Terry as he was doing this for us and the work we still had to do out there, if pallying up to Alton ensured that, then Jerry needed to support him.

"Listen, I accept that, yeah I know I shouldn't, but do you know how hard it is being left out like this and only being fed piecemeal, if I had my way I'd tell that two bit gangster where to shove it. But, Listen man, I understand, just frustrated wanna get back in there you know!"

I tried to calm him down but he was pacing up and down the bar like a caged animal gone feral. It couldn't be much longer, how long does it take for a cat to get bored of playing with the trapped mouse before he bites it head off. I assured Jerry that the latest news was good and we would soon be out there again.

A week later Terry called to set up a meeting, he had been given the green light by Alton and wanted to go over the plan with us. I arrived at the local just as Alton was leaving, we passed in the doorway, and he looked at me and flashed a gold toothed half smile at me and walked on. I sat down at our table and Terry got up to get me my usual. He sat back down and gave me my drink in the same movement.

He suggested we wait for Jerry, who, as usual, was late. I asked him what Alton was doing here; Terry explained that he was going over things to make sure I understood the plan and to reinforce his threat about the Torture Chamber. Terry said that he had to remind him that this was a business we knew well so he should be rest assured that nothing was going to go wrong. Then he dropped the bombshell;

"Yeah, and he wanted to come along wid us, I had to persuade him udder wise, it took a while but eventually he understand my point, den him want to have one ah him goons wid us. I tell him if dat is the case den he can keep his chamber and do de whole t'ing himself. He understand in de end, so it just us, like we like it."

Terry had read my mind; he knew that neither Jerry nor I would agree to Alton and or one of his goons being with us. This was our gig and he had to be content that we would do the job that he wanted; after all we were experts now. Even though Terry had said that he had persuaded him not to come with us I wasn't comfortable about the whole thing and tried to say to Terry that maybe we should drop the whole thing and go about our normal lives.

We had done what we had set out to do, the streets were safer, the bad lads had got a taste of their own medicine, we had given our community back its confidence, and we could finish it now and not be indebted to Alton or anyone else. Jerry arrived as I was in the middle of my sentence and punched me on the arm telling me to stop being so cautious.

"Listen, don't talk that way, this is just a setback, we do this job for him then we go back to how it was, we running t'ings! Listen, we got things on him, Terry knows how he operates so don't worry. We only just started man, come on!"

"Yeah man, don't fret so, once we do this for him I'll get him to back off. We do dis job and he'll have to be grateful, and we'll do it our way."

I told them that I wish I had their confidence, that it didn't feel right. We could easily tell him to get lost, pack up our costumes and tools and leave him to it. I just could not trust him and the last thing I want is to be in his pocket and both of them should think hard about it as well. There was no persuading them they were both confident and, anyway notwithstanding they both wanted to continue. I couldn't leave them on their own it was a three man job, I had to get these doubts out of my mind and get on with the job in hand, which they said was not finished, somewhere in the back of my mind I wished it was. I could see portents of danger hanging over us, a scythe dangling over our heads and this scythe was in the hands of Alton Weekes dressed in a pitch black robe...

SUPERNOVA chapter 16

The plan was very sketchy, Alton refused to give us a name or any other detail about the target, except where he would be in two days time. Apparently, according to Alton he was going to be in the car park of the local college sitting in a black Volkswagen Golf. That he would be with two other people a man and a woman, who will simply hand him over to us. I had to ask Terry to explain this some more because I was not liking the fact that someone else was simply going to hand this guy over to us, that we were going to be seen by others, something we should never agree to.

Terry tried to placate me saying that we would be in disguise and the others there will not recognise us at all. I remained uncomfortable with this and asked if Terry could talk with Alton to change this. Jerry was equally as reticent about this plan, we both agreed that there was no way that we could go ahead if this was the plan.

Terry phoned Alton and went outside the bar to discuss the sticking point. He was gone about ten minutes, in which time I tried to convince Jerry that we needed to be very careful about all this, that I could see everything crashing in around us. I told him that I didn't want us to charge in like the charge of the light brigade and all of us getting picked off by the enemy riflemen, something we were in danger of doing.

I wanted to tell him 'I quit!' but that would be to leave him and Terry alone and in the clutches of Alton Weekes. If they were going down I had to be with them, loyalty had to count for something especially with what we have all been through the past few months not to talk about the fact that we had been friends all our lives. I had to stay even if it was just to protect them, even if it was from themselves. Terry came back and explained a compromise to us.

"Weekesy has this plan where he is going to get this guy to meet him to 'talk' about what happened to his brother. He is going to set the meeting in the car park, but he will not be there because he may be followed. He will mek it so dat the couple will wait wid him until Weekes turns up, that way while they are waiting it will look like friends talking in a car and if our target is being followed by police they will lose interest in him, especially when they know Weekesy will be in a meeting with police at this same time. The plan now will be dat as we draw up into the car park the couple will tell dis guy that Weekes is in the back of the van and he should go now, they will explain that it has to be dis way in case police see dem together. He has no doubt he will go without a struggle, how we get him into the van is down to us, well what do you say?"

"Listen, that sounds a lot better, that couple will not see us cos we can park behind them on the bend where the turning point in the car park is. We can have the doors open by the time he gets to us, you Barry can then be out of the van and as he gets to the back get the sack over him and push him in to me."

It sounded like a plan, no-one will then be able to make out who we were, just one guy in a white van and then we will be off job done. It all sounded too easy, but I could not find a flaw in the plan so agreed to it. The good thing was Alton would be with the police so he would now not insist on being present. We were alone to do things our way, which might mean we could actually save a life.

The two days seemed to take an eternity to come round, time seemed to have slowed and sometimes even felt like it had stopped altogether. I was having some very bad dreams about this job and would wake up in the early hours of the morning sweating, then I would be unable to go back to sleep. I went through the plan, over and over again trying to tie down any little inconsistency any idiosyncrasy, it had to be perfectly executed. But I kept having premonitions; my dreams, my visions, kept telling me something different, that we were destined for a disaster, that the dark clouds I kept seeing over all three of us indicated our end. In my dream someone was laughing whilst we fell in unison, one hand clutching our chests the other reaching for the dark cloud, looking up I saw Alton Weekes' smoking gun in his left hand and holding someone's severed head in his right hand, laughing as he looked down on us saying;

"I love it when a plan comes together, ha, ha, ha ha!"

I didn't want to die that's why it was so important to execute this thing properly and leave nothing to chance. But, if I was going to die then at least it would be next to the two people I loved next to my family. Over the next two days I rang Terry and Jerry constantly going over the plan and making sure that there were no other changes.

On D day I insisted on us meeting early just to go through it all again. I tried to persuade them to do a dummy run but they put their foot down at that and tried to get me to relax, assuring me that everything would be alright, 'smooth' was the word Terry used, 'smooth' was the last adjective I would have used to describe how I felt all this would go. It felt to me like when were kids riding our home made bike with no brakes on a rocky, winding path going downhill fast with nothing to stop us riding over the precipice.

The time came to set off to the rendezvous point, I sat in the back and pulled on my mask and hat and got my sack at the ready. Jerry sat with me, he seemed cool and ready for any action, I wished I was, but the feelings of fear and dread remained with me. I felt the van come to an abrupt halt and Terry calling us to be ready as we had arrived. Jerry opened the back doors and I jumped out and stood sack at the ready on the blind side of the intended victim.

It seemed like forever before he reached the van, as he took his first cautious glimpse into the back of the van I leapt from my hiding place and threw the sack over his head and pushed him hard into the van. Simultaneously Jerry had grabbed him and pulled him head first into the van then began tying him up. I jumped into the van then slammed the doors shut as Terry sped away towards the Torture Chamber, rare groove music spilling from the stereo.

Throughout the whole journey this guy covered by a sack and tethered like a goat going to slaughter never moved, never made a sound. I had to prod him every now and again to make sure that he was still alive. Unusually Jerry hadn't started beating him; he sat in the corner simply looking at the tethered bundle. It looked as if he was trying to work something out, some mad equation that had got him puzzled on the journey home from work on the tube.

Jerry mumbled something that I couldn't quite hear, I asked him to repeat it but he just shook his head and carried on staring at the victim lying motionless on the floor. I felt the van pull to a halt, heard the engine turn off and the music stop simultaneously. Terry swung the doors to the van open then went to open the doors to the Torture Chamber. I had to shout at Jerry to help me get the victim out of the van.

Inside the chamber I untied the knot that Jerry had made holding him in the sack took the sack off him and pushed him into the chair at the table in the middle of the room. Terry turned on the light above the table, light cascaded over the victim lighting up his face, he squinted in the bright light and blinked his eyes many times stopping when his eyes had become accustomed to the light.

Jerry had walked over to the tool table and we could hear the clinking, clanking and thudding as he set about re-arranging the tool table. I looked at the victim's face, I half recognised him but couldn't place where I had seen him. I looked into his eyes, expecting to see fear, after all he had killed a gangland leader's brother, surely after we had snatched him he must be scared for his life, but he just looked back at me nothing in his eyes or his face. It surprised me and scared me, this guy was sitting there expecting, and waiting for death, Alton really did do a number on him.

Terry struck the first blow a crushing left hook to his right temple, which sent his head bobbing from left to right, he followed this up with a straight southpaw jab exploding his nose and sent blood showering over me. Terry then grabbed him by the hair and pulled his head as far back as it could go, and began to explain to him why he was here and what he could expect to happen to him.

He snarled at him how he had taken a life and he was about to find out how it felt to be powerless, how we had taken control of his body, and began describing the things that we were going to do to it. He then told him that we were not going to kill him but that he is going to wish for death once we had finished with him. He then whispered to him how his life as he knew it before had now ended that he was moving into a life of pain courtesy of the Weekes family. Nothing came back the victim simply looked up at Terry as if to say do your worse.

Jerry had come up behind me armed with a large spanner and the large pliers. Suddenly there was a loud noise as he dropped the tools to the floor and rushed over to the victim, holding back Terry's right arm just as he was aiming another punch at the victim's unguarded nose.

"Listen, stop no more I know this guy, he's Nelsons friend, Nelson's girlfriends brother, what the fuck is going on?"

He looked at the victim and began wiping the blood from his face.

"Listen, Tyrone isn't it? What the fuck are you doing here did you kill Weekes' brother, what about Nelson, where is Nelson?"

He began shaking Tyrone urging him to tell him that Nelson was safe, that he had nothing to do with this.

"Listen guys I've got to go and find Nelson make sure he's safe God knows if Weekes has got to him and what he's done to him, I've got to go!"

With that he started for the door, I held him back telling him that he couldn't just leave us here with Tyrone and anyway where was he going on foot, that we would drive him and we will take Tyrone with us. There was no way that we could do anything to him now we knew who he was. Terry had started to untie his hands, when suddenly the door flew open and in walked Alton Weekes, he was on his own no bodyguard just him and he had something in his hand his face was contorted with rage and he was shouting something. I couldn't hear what it was all I could see was my nightmare of the previous night turning into reality, I could even feel the dark cloud over my head.

"Why the fucking hell are you untying him, why aren't you beating him, you're supposed to be beating him. I knew you fuckers would fuck up that's why I'm here I'm gonna finish it and then I'm gonna finish you guys, you're all fucking dead!"

"Weekes man, put the piece down you ain't gonna do shit, this is Jerry's boys mate we ain't gonna let you touch him and we're all walking out of here."

"Listen, I'm sorry for your loss, but if you do this guy you're going after my son I can't let you do that, just leave it, please?"

I couldn't move I was in a state of shock looking down the barrel of a gun; I was going to die in this God forsaken place with a silly mask on my face. I could hear Terry and Jerry try to reason with him, but the gun remained aimed at us. Weekes demanded that Jerry and Terry move out of his way and if they didn't he'll shoot him through them.

Then Tyrone began to speak he didn't talk to anyone in particular, he began telling the story of what happened starting with Everton molesting Salisha almost raping her, how he would have done if the police hadn't been called, how she had put up a spirited fight. He described the day he and Nelson got the truth out of her and how he felt as she told him what had happened. He then looked directly at Alton and asked him if that was his sister what would he have done, would that guy still be walking.

"Fuck you, fuck you, he was my brother man, I had to watch my mother grieve like nothing before, she had hopes for him that he wouldn't live the life me and the others lived, that he would make her proud. She loved him; I hated her for that cos she could never love me the same way. I got to do this for her; she'll love me when I tell her that I've avenged his death, now you two fuck off out the way."

He aimed his gun at Tyrone and got ready to shoot him. He squeezed the trigger, Jerry jumped on top of Tyrone and the bullet hit Jerry at the top of his left shoulder with a sickening thud. Blood began to seep like a river of molten lava from the hole left by the bullet. Jerry screamed in pain and slumped into Tyrone's lap breathing heavily and gasping for air. Tyrone was also screaming as the bullet had passed through Jerry and hit his right arm with force breaking the skin and landing on the floor with a metallic clinking sound.

I could see Weekes walking forward towards Tyrone and Jerry getting ready to aim at Tyrone's head when another shot rang out. The coat Weekes was wearing billowed to the sound and he turned to his left hand side to see Terry pointing a gun at him. Weekes looked shocked for a moment then he slumped to his knees holding his left hand side with his right hand, then moving his right hand into his line of vision, it was smeared with blood.

"You cunt, you shot me why the fuck did you do that?"

He tried to raise the pistol to fire another shot but he couldn't it wouldn't move, he swore again then lurched forward then fell sideways his right hand still holding where the bullet had entered. By this time Jerry had also rolled out of Tyrone's lap and onto the floor. I looked at the carnage in front of me and still I couldn't move. Terry was walking towards me shouting my name, I could see him getting closer to me the gun was still in his hand. I cowered behind my hands and shouted at him not to shoot me.

"Don't be so fucking stupid, come on man snap out of it we gotta do something, we gotta get dese guys to hospital or something, raasclaat, fucking shit, dis is a fucking mess!"

I couldn't agree with him more, but he was right we had to do something. This isn't how it was supposed to be, we had a mission, fate had bestowed it on us. Only now it felt like fate had given us a dummy hand, set us up. I certainly didn't think things would end like this, I had felt noble like I was ordained by a higher power to flex my muscles and brainpower to devise such a thing. Now things seem to be crumbling around me my pedestal has been knocked and now I am teetering on the brink waiting to fall off, but scrambling hard to find my balance and stay upright. I have now to find a way to stay upright and see this plan through to the end, whatever that may be.

Something snapped inside my head and I moved into advocate mode, I told Terry to bring the van right up to the doors, I will tend to these guys and see if I could do anything for them. I went first to Jerry who was motionless on the floor, there was a lot of blood but he was still breathing, I looked around for something to stem the blood, nothing was around and what there was I couldn't use.

I ripped off some of my overall and tried to wad it onto the bullet hole, but there was too much blood and two holes. Tyrone was begging me to finish untying him as he could help, he said he wasn't hurt bad as Jerry had taken the full force of the bullet. I untied him and told him to see to Jerry. I went over to Alton, I checked his pulse it was still strong. Again, there was a pool of blood where he lay, his breathing was laboured but he was alive. Terry came back and said the van was in position and Alton's car was there as well.

"Terry we've got to put Jerry and Alton in Alton's car and get them as close as possible to the Hospital, we can't put them in the van as that would be too conspicuous. I tell you what, get them in his car and I'll drive it, you and Tyrone can follow me so that I can jump in with you once I've got them into the hospital at least, got to be fast cos they are both losing a lot of blood, come on you two let's get them into the car."

Terry and Tyrone lifted Alton and squeezed him into the back of the Porsche, there wasn't much room but at least he got in. I dragged Jerry and placed him as gently as possible into the front seat.

"Terry turn off the light and lock the doors then follow me to the hospital."

He did as I said then I was off, as fast as I could go without attracting the attention of police out to stop joy riders in a nice fast car. My only concern was to get Jerry to hospital, I couldn't care less about Weekes he lived by the gun so if he died by one it would be sort of poetic, another Weekes dying for the life he lived. But Jerry didn't deserve this he was a decent man who cared about his family and the community in which he lived so much so he was prepared to put his life on the line for it. The Star Chamber was over, finished, like in my dreams. If we got through this then I will be so happy to go back to my normal, mundane, uninteresting life.

As it was late there weren't too many people about and the car parks were almost empty. I looked around for somewhere to park the car and for a plan to come to my mind. I had got them here without a hitch, but how am I going to get them seen without anyone noticing me. I could see Terry behind me he had caught up at last. I wound the window down and told him to park up in the car park, I had a plan.

The Accident and Emergency department was at the bottom of a slight incline, if I could get Alton into the drivers seat I could turn off the engine, leave the hand brake off and roll the car down to the Accident and Emergency department, the sound of the car hitting something, anything should attract people's attention and I can be in the van before anyone thought to look up in my direction.

Getting Alton into the front seat was hard, but I managed it, I also managed to get a lot of his blood on me. I leaned over and checked Jerry he was still breathing but he was out for the count. I took the hand brake off, the car didn't move. I had to get behind it and push it with all my might, then I stood and watched as it rolled down the incline and smashed into a parked car directly outside the entrance to Accident and Emergency. I turned and began to walk quickly to the car park where Terry was waiting for me. I could hear people shouting and the sound of a car alarm whirring in the distance, I didn't look back I just kept right on walking. I jumped into the van.

"Is it done?"

"Yep it's done let's hope that he's okay!"

We set off and passed near to Accident and Emergency we could see all the commotion with doctors and nurses rushing about around the car and the few people who were at the hospital, milling around, craning their necks to see the latest victims of gangland violence, or just to see blood and shot up bodies. None of us spoke apart from Terry to ask Tyrone where he lived.

We got to the address he had given it was only then that I noticed his arm was bleeding, I told him that he needed to get it seen too. I got out the van to let him out as he got out I said to him that he should keep quiet about what happened tonight, that he couldn't tell Nelson or anyone that he had been involved in all this. I told him to let Jerry tell Nelson whatever he needed to tell him, that if he ever needs someone to talk to just ask for me or Terry. I watched as he ran into his house then went back to the van.

"Mate, that's it I can't do this anymore, it's all messed up. Jerry's half dead, Alton Weekes probably dead how many others are going to die because of us?"

"How many are going to die because we've stopped?"

"So you're saying that we should continue?"

"We've gone this far, I can't lose Jerry for nothing and I can't believe that all this is for nothing. If Weekes is out the way then we are ahead and clear, no-one can touch us. If Jerry goes then we do it for him, but we can't just stop now!"

The path of the righteous is beset on all sides by the inequalities of the selfish and the tyranny of evil men. We had walked the path and steered a path through this. We had sought out those that threatened and harmed our brothers and visited them with great vengeance and furious anger. One of ours had been hurt but many more of our brothers had been saved. Are we our brothers' keepers?

THE END

Lightning Source UK Ltd.
Milton Keynes UK
27 November 2010

163526UK00001B/53/P